YELLOW BEAR LODGE

YELLOW BEAR LODGE

A Montana Dude Ranch Adventure

Bryant C. Blewett
and
Ellen Marshall

SUNSTONE PRESS

SANTA FE

The events, people, and incidents in this story are the
sole product of the author's imagination. The story is
fictional and any resemblance to individuals
living or dead is purely coincidental.

Sunstone books may be purchased for educational, business,
or sales promotional use. For information please write:
Special Markets Department, Sunstone Press,
P.O. Box 2321, Santa Fe, New Mexico 87504-2321.

Library of Congress Cataloging-in-Publication Data:

Blewett, Bryant C.
    Yellow Bear Lodge : a Montana dude ranch adventure / by
    Bryant C.Blewett and Ellen Marshall.
        p. cm.
    ISBN 0-86534-412-4 (pbk.)
    1. Dude ranches—Fiction. 2. Grizzly bear—Fiction.
    3. Montana—Fiction. I. Marshall, Ellen, 1952- II. Title.

PS3602.L49 Y45 2004
813'.6—dc22

                                    2003021085

Published in
SUNSTONE PRESS
POST OFFICE BOX 2321
SANTA FE, NM 87504-2321 / USA
(505) 988-4418 / ORDERS ONLY (800) 243-5644
FAX (505) 988-1025
WWW.SUNSTONEPRESS.COM

To Ron and Phyllis
who made the journey
on the dude ranch trail possible.

CONTENTS

BELOW ZERO

There is nothing colder than Montana in February when the Arctic wind starts to blow across the prairie through the northern wheat fields east of Conrad. The flat wheat land extends as far as you can see. There is no physical border between Canada and the United States, just pure, flat, frozen Arctic prairie. You can stand on the hood of your car and see the earth curve to the east. Sitting out in the middle of 10,000 acres of 65 bushel an acre wheat land, is a ranch house. Not what you normally think of as a ranch house, it's made of pumice blocks designed in a rectangle. It's 120 feet long by 30 feet wide, two stories high. Both the top and bottom story are exactly the same dimensions. The only difference is, the bottom story is underground. This house was designed to stand up against the Arctic winds that travel unabated from Hudson Bay directly through the Montana prairie.

The top story has an elegant living room with three bedrooms off to the western side. On the eastern side is a kitchen, bathroom, kid's room and a stairway downstairs. The downstairs is furnished with a pool table, a lavish bar, three bedrooms on the western side, a shower, bathroom, and a battery room where the windmill outside produces power to recharge the batteries. It belongs to Wendy and Wade Wolf.

Wade handled the Suburban with care. The gravel road was icy and at 35 degrees below zero danger lurked on either side of the barrow pits. With a flick of an ear and the flash of an eye a deer could leap out from the dark and quickly destroy a vehicle. An injured person would die of exposure.

The school board meeting had broken up early and Wade was looking forward to seeing his family.

Wendy had been married before to a guy from Minnesota and had a son, Canyon. Widowed early, she had married Wade twelve years ago when she got pregnant with their daughter, a little girl with golden wheat-like hair named Harvest. He loved those kids. They meant everything to him. He felt as protective as a she-wolf and wondered if other fathers ever felt that way. He guessed it was because of the lack of mothering they got from Wendy. Wade had been concerned about Wendy's drinking for a long time. This winter she had been drinking in town more than ever. Since Canyon had gotten his driver's license and could chauffeur Harvest to all her activities, Wendy spent a lot more time in town with her friends. She frequently came home drunk.

Jamming the Suburban into four-wheel drive low, Wade broke through the snowdrift at the entrance to his driveway. There were tracks ahead of his on the driveway but almost covered by fresh snow. Wonder who that could be, Wade thought. As he turned toward the garage, a pickup he didn't recognize was parked in the driveway. It made the hair on the back of his neck stand up. Wendy's drinking had been getting worse and worse. He never knew what she would do next.

The snow crunched under his feet as he made his way up to the closed-in porch. Stepping inside he removed his boots and winter coat and noticed another man's boots and coat hanging on the wall. Wade shouted a greeting, "Hello, I'm home!"

Harvest and Canyon immediately replied from the living room, "Hi Dad! We're in here." The TV was loud and tuned to a sitcom.

"Hi, guys. Where's your mom?"

"Downstairs with a new friend," they replied. They kept their eyes glued to the TV, afraid of his reaction.

"When did they get here," Wade asked.

"Before we got home from school. Mom told us to stay upstairs and watch television," Harvest replied.

Opening the door as he started down the stairs, Wade's heart began to speed up. He knew something was wrong. The pool table was empty as was the bar. A half bottle of Jack Daniels sat alone on the counter. Laughter floated out from the big middle bedroom. Wade stopped and commanded himself to get under control.

Through the open door he could see Wendy naked with a strange naked man kneeling over her. He lowered himself slowly and she groaned with pleasure. Wade's mind flashed white with anger. He couldn't see or hear. He stepped forward and his arm flashed out hitting the door with all of his force, slamming it shut like a rifle shot. It had been rumored she had done this before, but never in their home. His marriage was over.

Taking the stairs two at a time he slammed the stairway door behind him and turned to Harvest and Canyon coming down the hall. As soon as he saw the kids, his anger faded to sorrow. They were more important than anything else.

"Please get your overnight stuff together. We're going to stay in town tonight."

"Oh Dad, please? We don't want to go," Harvest said.

"Do it now! I'll wait for you in the Suburban."

Wade walked out on the porch. There wasn't any wind that night and the snow crunched underneath his feet as he walked to the car. The cold night moon glowed like a giant pearl hung in the sky. He prayed, "What can I do to make my life better?" He thought back to his Crow Indian ancestors and prayed to Mother Earth. "Take me; take me to where I may be happy with my children." Looking at the full moon reflecting off the snow over mile after mile of wheat fields, a warm Chinook wind began to blow. He turned his back to feel the warmth. Maybe Mother Earth had heard his prayer.

The kids came crunching through the snow. "Why are we going to town," Canyon asked.

"I'll explain in the car," he said as he threw their duffles into the back seat.

INTERVIEWS

Yellow Bear Lodge was a complete contrast to the frozen wheat ranch in northern Montana. Wade's new home was 300 miles south on the east side of the Absaroka-Beartooth Wilderness. In a beautiful pine tree lined valley at 6,400 feet where spring arrives in early June, wildflowers covered the meadows as far as you could see. Deer, elk, and moose used Yellow Bear's horse pastures to have their babies in the spring. Wobbly legged calves took their first shaky steps under the watchful eyes of their mothers. Within days they were able to cross the rushing Boulder River where schools of trout rose to catch a mayfly hatch. About this time both the black and grizzly bears made their appearance in the upper meadows of the valley, rolling over rocks to reach for the grubs they fed on while they began their annual migration up to the high, cool alpine valleys.

Human beings had been living in this valley on this very spot for 11,500 years. Within a few miles west of the ranch, the mountains opened up into three different drainages that converged and blended into the Boulder River. These three drainages, the Boulder River, Meatrack and Silver Lake, offered the native hunters the ability to shelter their families in this quiet valley for weeks while they hunted obsidian up the Boulder River into Yellowstone. In Meatrack they hunted elk and dried the strips of meat into jerky. The Silver Lake trail led them through moose and bear country and once over the mountain range, to a natural hot springs. The "hunting rock" used by prehistoric men for a blind for killing mountain sheep sat atop a rise in the horse pasture. The ring of rocks used to hold the blind in place could still be seen today.

The rock cliffs that rose 300 feet above the pasture were a favorite lookout for the hunter/warriors. Today, the guests enjoyed the same views through the huge picture windows of the rustic Yellow Bear Lodge.

Anything that moved in or out of the valley could be seen from here. The warriors idled away their afternoons chipping out arrowheads and spear points from the obsidian while looking out for horse thieves. The stately tipis stood one by one below on the valley floor, their banners waving gently in the breeze. They were within easy walking distance of the sparkling river which became a backdrop to the horse pasture where their herd of Appaloosa and mountain horses grazed.

Atop the 300 foot cliff, Yellow Bear Lodge offered five picture windows for a 180 degree view from the dining and living room. The four lodge rooms sat on top of the lodge whose balcony offered the same spectacular view that the warriors enjoyed while they made their arrowheads.

Yellow Bear Ranch consisted of a lodge, three cabins, a bunkhouse, a trailer house and a washhouse all strung along the back side of the cliff. In the 1800s the land was homesteaded by an ambitious pioneer and 160 acres of the levelest land was drawn up. He used the property for raising cattle in the summer and as an overnight rest stop for bands of sheep as they made their annual trip from the west Boulder valley to the alpine meadows high above. One of the changes that had occurred was the upgrading of the road which allowed motorized vehicles instead of just horses and wagons. Little else has changed. Beautiful mountains reaching 10,000 feet to the sky still protected the valley. Green Douglas Fir and Lodgepole pines whispered in the wind as their neighbors, the aspen, fluttered their sparkling leaves in the sun. The Boulder River ran crystal clear with the sun reflecting off of the red, green, black and gold bottom. Above the rush of the river you could hear the quiet.

The ranch opens mid-May and closes mid-November when winter turns the mountains into a wonderland for wild animals. The deer and elk feed without fear and the coyotes howl at the moon.

Two years later, Wade Wolf woke up as a single father on this guest ranch in the wilderness, 40 miles from the closest town. The owners were looking for someone to manage the ranch. He applied, along with several other people. His ability to handle horses and people and the degree he got in recreation management from Montana State University, got him the job. As he struggled through the divorce, the fights and the alcoholism, he decided this was what he really wanted. If his children would ever forgive him, this would be an ideal place to have them come live with him. He had only seen them sporadically the last two years, but had written to them nearly every week. So he told the two owners, "I'll run your place. It's not very big, but with twenty guests a week and eight employees, I can make it pay."

Now all he needed were paying guests and enough help to run the ranch. He placed an ad in the local papers for employees. After receiving several calls, he set up a series of interviews at the Four Corners Café.

Marie Katerina Bearwalks was a 5'4" bundle of human energy, combining one quarter Crow Indian, one quarter Mexican-Aztec, and the fiery temper of one half Portuguese. She had a round figure with the grace of a deer. Her outstanding features were her brown eyes, her black hair, and her skin, the color of a newborn fawn that felt like satin. Men loved to touch it. In most cases, couldn't resist. The problem was that Marie liked them to touch it. She would fall in love quickly, and based on her strong Catholic background, would marry. Marie loved her family. She was the third of six children. Her father was a half Crow Indian, half Mexican, steel worker. Her mother was a full blooded Portuguese and supplemented the household income by working lunches and baking on the side. Marie inherited her mother's interest in baking and loved to cook.

In her first 33 years of life, Marie had been married four times. With her first husband, Bob, she had a daughter, June, who was being raised by Bob and his new wife, in Texas. Her second and third marriages were brief encounters lasting six and nine months. Her last husband, Kirk Rudbeck, was the Scandinavian blue-eyed Viking she had always dreamed about. He ran an outfitting business in the Bob Marshall Wilderness and owned a thousand acres near Depuyer. The marriage was fine for the first two years. However, it soon became obvious that Kirk's jealousy was the kind that leads to violence. One time in the Bob Marshall Wilderness when Marie was flirting with a new Eastern client as she was cooking, she saw Kirk glaring furiously at her. He had been drinking with clients. There is nowhere to run in the wilderness and when he caught her alone, he hit her hard, several times. It was over a week before they returned from the wilderness and her friends never realized how badly she had been hurt. She went directly to a lawyer in Great Falls, and began divorce proceedings. Kirk fought the divorce and it was only in the last month that the divorce was final and Kirk was no longer in her life.

With Kirk behind her, it was time to move on and that meant finding a new job. She noticed the ad in the AgriNews and applied for a job at the Yellow Bear Lodge. Driving along Interstate 90 on a sunny spring day, the Montana mountains crystal clear in the background, the sun reflected off her new belt with its shiny buckle that wrapped around her dress with the Indian print that she loved so much. Marie's mind focused on the Four Corners Café and her interview with Wade Wolf. Along with her new boots, she felt good about herself and knew she'd make a good impression. She knew that she had all the right credentials to become the best cook Yellow Bear Lodge ever had.

Sitting in a corner, Wade Wolf checked his watch and glanced out the window at the Crazy Mountains. He enjoyed this process of interviewing at his favorite table at the Four Corners. He never knew what new and exciting people would walk into his life. Hiring the staff for a guest ranch was always full of surprises.

As Marie walked in the door, she looked across the room and saw a young, handsome man looking wistfully out the window.

I'll get this job, she thought, and quickly crossing the room, she held out her hand. "Good afternoon, Mr. Wolf."

"Howdy, ma'am. Glad you could make it." Taking her hand firmly, but softly, he felt an electric shock that caused his heart to miss a beat. His green eyes flashed as he looked deeply into her dark eyes. The emotional reaction caused each of them to half close their eyes in that cat-like expression which means, "I like you and can trust you." The handshake lasted two heartbeats longer that it should have and Marie, for the life of her, couldn't remember what she said in the interview, until Wade mentioned her starting date. "Will May fifteenth be okay for you to start ma'am?"

"Of course," Marie answered suddenly with a start. "I'll need directions and we should get together again to plan how we will be buying the produce."

"We can go over the produce with the Sysco manager on the fifteenth right here in town and then you can follow me to the ranch, not that you can get lost. It's a dead-end road," he said.

As Marie left she was thinking, I can't get involved with another man! No way! I'm going to give up men and become celibate the rest of my life. I never, ever want a man in my life again.

The minute Wade looked up from her resume as she walked across the room, he knew this was his new cook. She had everything the ranch required. Wilderness cooking experience, Culinary Academy in Billings and several summers dealing with ranch guests. But nowhere in that resume did it say anything about how she looked and carried herself like an Indian princess with beautiful straight black hair, dark brown eyes and skin that made you want to stroke it. From the minute she spoke in that soft quiet voice, he knew he was in trouble. Once he touched her and felt the electricity, he felt like running away. No, he thought, I'm not having any more women in my life. Now that I'm divorced, I'm never, ever going to touch a woman again. This woman's going to be the ranch cook and nothing else. Still, it will be nice having her around. She brings the right qualities of professionalism and American Native culture to the ranch. He gave Marie instructions on how to find the Sysco manager on May 15th. She smiled back at him as she walked out the door.

Wade flipped the page for his next interview for a head wrangler. So far, he'd seen four men with very good backgrounds, but none of them had the right feel. Wade thought, what the ranch needs is someone who loves horses and understands them as individuals. Horses that enjoy their jobs, which enjoy being ridden, should be handled gently, with tender loving care. The Yellow Bear Lodge horses enjoyed their jobs.

Just then the door banged open and in walked his next interview, Cindy Tucker. Hat in hand, cowboy boots, western jeans and scarf, she had a big smile with the sun flashing off her large even teeth. "Howdy, Sir!" she said, shaking Wade's hand with a strong, firm grip.

"Howdy Ma'am," he replied. "I see you grew up on a ranch around here."

"Yup, not far from where you winter your horses, the Patterson's old place. My folks bought it back in the fifties."

"I see you were a wrangler in Arizona. Why did you leave?"

"Mr. Wolf, sir, have you ever been to Arizona? It's hot. Too damn hot for this Montana girl! I bet hell is even cooler. They don't have to build a fire to barbecue. They just hang the food in midair and wait ten minutes. It's got cactus, snakes, scorpions, ants, spiders, flies and no water! I grew up in these mountains where water is everywhere. In Montana when it gets hot, we mean eighty five degrees. When we say cool at night, we mean cool at night. Besides, I got homesick so I gave that fancy dude ranch my notice, and headed home!" Barely taking a breath she continued, "Did ya know I know your horses? Your winter range is right next to my parent's place. You don't know this, but every time I came home, I would visit your herd. One night, I even slept with them and I know all their names. Do you know that they miss people? They need someone to talk to them in the winter. On nice days, I even rode Joe bareback. Do you know that Dixie, that new horse, has a puncture on her right flank? I put some salve on it last week. It looked okay this morning. When can I start?"

Wade just smiled. That's the right horse feeling. With her sense of humor she will surely get along with the guests, he thought. He answered, "It looks like you've already started." And that's how Cindy Tucker began her long career as head wrangler of Yellow Bear Lodge. Wade instructed Cindy to find herself a junior wrangler, giving her a general description and emphasizing the need for a person who would respect horses and get along with people.

Years ago, the ranch owners had hired Anna Wilson, the head housekeeper. Each year she would bring two college coeds from Bozeman with her when she arrived on May 15th. She was extremely organized. In the spring, she packed her Forest Service husband off for the summer, hired the two helpers, jumped in her pickup truck and arrived at the ranch in plenty of time to have the place spotless before the first guests arrived. Her dependability took a lot of pressure off Wade during the opening days of the season.

This left Wade with only one major gap to fill in his summer staff, the maintenance man. Now Wade thought, if I could only find a maintenance guy who could double as a jeep driver, float boat operator and fall hunting guide. He had seen several, but most of them were either derelicts or rejects from AA. But he was feeling hopeful. His next interview was with Ben Johnson. Ben had driven garbage trucks for Miles City, skinned buffalo hides one winter for the Crow Indians, was currently working in an electrical plumbing supply store, and like most Montanans, held down at least three jobs a year. He had even run a trap line in the Absaroka-Beartooth Wilderness, not far from Yellow Bear Lodge. Ben walked in sure and solid, a tall mountain man. He had a big knife, black hat and shirt, and an easy gait that covered the distance across the room in three strides. "Howdy, sir."

"Howdy, Ben. I'm looking for a maintenance man plus someone to drive our jeep into the high country."

"Well, sir, I can drive anything and I can fix just about anything. I know your mountains better than the animals. If you're needing to check on my skills, ask your old pal, Ted Wolverton, at the Conoco. I've been helping him on weekends and we just finished with your Suburban. You'll have to watch the back shocks. They're about to go."

"Why are you working weekends?"

"I needed extra money to pay off my debts. My old lady ran off with some guy to South Dakota and without her paycheck it's been tight. We were together almost ten years. She wanted kids, and I guess I can't or I wasn't home long enough, but when I was home, I sure tried like hell! Anyway, I don't blame her. What about the job?"

"We start up the mountain on the fifteenth, Wade said, with a smile in his heart.

JAKE AND THE HORSES

Jake thought, what a wonderful job this is! Cindy Tucker is a great boss. She's more of a friend than a boss. I'm through with that 10,000 acre ranch out of Roundup where my two older brothers and father still argue and fight. Ever since my Mom died, seems like I never had anyone to talk to. All I did was chores. I'm glad I left. Never would I have guessed that I would be sitting here on this rock, overlooking this beautiful green valley where my ancestors fished, hunted and grazed their horses. Up there in that high meadow at 8,000 feet, they hunted elk, moose, bear, and deer. I remember my grandfather telling the stories his grandfather told him about the legend of the yellow bears. Now I work at the ranch, Yellow Bear Lodge, which was named after the legend. Not bad for an eighteen year old.

Angelica is behind me now. Oh, I loved her but she never cared. How long did I wait to ask her out? Three years? No, that's not right. I asked her out my freshman year and she turned me down. When I finally got my nerve up again, I was a senior at Roundup High, and everyone knew I had a crush on her and was planning on asking her out. After a month of planning, I finally did. She said, "Yes," right away with a funny smile. We arranged to meet at seven pm in front of the Vicar Drug and Sundries. Of course, I arrived early in my new jeans and shirt, hat that I had brushed, buckle that I had polished and boots shined. I even smelled good. Six-thirty waited, six-forty-five, waited. Seven o'clock. She ought to be here soon. Seven-fifteen, waited. Seven-thirty waited. Seven forty-five, waited. Eight o'clock, an hour late. Something must have happened and she couldn't get away. I'll use the pay phone and call.

Just then the red and white Chevy with the fancy white fins came around the corner. It was Jim's, the football hero, captain of the team. There was Angelica sitting next to him with a big smile. She got out of the car walked up to me and planted a big sticky kiss on my lips. "Sorry I'm late," she whispered in my ear, "I had to give Jim a blow job first. Goodby sucker!"

She turned and jumped back in the car as Jim burned rubber down the street. I was shocked. How could anyone be so hateful? Would the earth open up so I could disappear? No. I couldn't cry, couldn't run. Just stood there, dropped my head so my cowboy hat covered my face. At eight-thirty I walked slowly up the street. The longest walk of my life. The one thought that gave strength to my legs was that the two of them deserved each other, a jerk and a cocksucker. I'm better than that. I will never, ever allow a woman to touch my feelings like that again.

Even today sitting here on the rock, I can still feel how humiliated, crushed, depressed and angry I felt. The mountains would be my love. The elk, moose, deer, bear, mountain lion, bobcat, all the birds and squirrels would be my family. I always wanted to have a big family.

Jake shook his head quickly as he heard a branch crack. He looked up just in time to see one of the most dangerous animals of the springtime step out of the trees. A mother moose was leading her newborn calf from the birthing place down to the pond near the river. The poor little calf could barely stand, much less walk. Its four skinny legs all trying to go in a different direction at once, it couldn't be over a week old. Mother Moose would walk about 25 feet ahead, turn, walk back two strides, lick the calf's face and start off again. Jake watched with a huge smile on his face as it took the mother and calf 30 minutes to navigate the 200 yards from the forest to the pond. Jake never moved a muscle. He valued his life. A mother moose can kill quicker than a grizzly bear, and run a lot faster.

A hand touched Jake's shoulder. He jumped. It was Cindy Tucker holding her fingers to her lips. "Shhh. Sorry, I just wanted you to know I was here," she whispered. "That mother moose was really beautiful but very dangerous. Jake, how did you find my favorite spot on the ranch so soon? You've only been here a day."

"Sorry, ma'am, I won't ever come here again," he stammered as he lowered his eyes.

"No, no, it's okay. Let's watch the moose and her calf and I'll tell you about the horses we're going to bring up tomorrow." They sat quietly for 45 minutes.

Then Cindy began her story. "You see, Jake, the horses come down that road from the corral every night. We'll turn them loose right before dinner at about five-thirty. We let them out of the corral and like good kids they head, clomp, clomp, clomp, down to the gate to the big pasture. Now if they don't make the turn into the gate, there's nothing to stop them for twenty-five miles. So for the first week or so, you'll have to ride down by the gate and show them the way. They come in two's, three's and four's until all twenty of them are in the pasture. They have such a good time they kick up their heels and roll in the dirt, talk about who rode them and whatever else horses talk about. One year we were holding them in the corral for about a week because the forest service wouldn't let us use our big pasture because it was being used by the elk, deer and moose for calving. The horses broke out of the corral because they were so excited to get into this big pasture. They looked like kids getting out of school for the summer. Jake, look over there in the trees. There are three mother elk with their calves right now!," she continued. "All the horses have their own names and personalities. You'll get to know them fast!"

THE ROAD

The road to the ranch is 42 miles of two lane highway. The last 17 miles is all gravel and sometimes one lane. It begins in Big Timber, the last gas and civilization where you can do all your errands by walking down one street. The post office, the Book Nook, the flyfishing store, Ace Hardware, the liquor store, and of course several bars along the way where you can have lunch. You know you're going too fast on the pavement when your head hits the ceiling and your beer spills in your lap because the car has just sailed through a patch of pavement where the permafrost has dropped the road like a roller coaster.

On the road today is Wade's nemesis, Shirley Van Holdenhouse, the Forest Service Agent. She is driving up the road on a bright spring day to see Wade. She's excited because she knows Wade is one of the most eligible bachelors on the Boulder. She has done everything she can to get him to ask her out. But Wade, still suffering from the divorce, is holding back, although he is a good dancer and good looking at 6'4", 220 pounds. But Shirley Van Holdenhouse is persistent and well, aggressive; the Forest Service type. She's 32, never had kids, been married twice, loves the outdoors and she's quite proud of her long blond hair and her gorgeous figure. Many men think she looks best in tight jeans. But her first love is the Forest Service green, and it is her duty to keep people like Wade in line so he doesn't violate any of the numerous rules she has been taught over the years.

Early morning found her leaving the Forest Service office in Big Timber and following the Boulder River as it wound along next to large alfalfa fields. Early spring mornings in Montana always bring the deer and the antelope out to feed side by side with the sheep and cattle. Along this stretch of the valley the river is wide and deep and it's only a few miles from where it flows into the Yellowstone.

Sixteen miles up the road Shirley passes the Road Kill Café. A hot springs road house from the 1930s to the 1960s with wild fraternity parties, gambling and whores, it had fallen onto quieter times ever since they moved it a mile down the road from McLeod. The Road Kill is a Quonset hut with wood paneling, bullet holes, beer stains, and a long "L" shaped bar that has been repaired several times due to excessive weight when people danced on top of it. The blood stains, scuff marks, knife cuts and spur gouges still remain. The porch was added about 10 years ago, making room for two picnic tables and a sturdy 2"x6" railing where on any Friday or Saturday night, you could view 10 to 20 sets of buns all in tight jeans. The bands were never memorable but the local characters were.

Leprechaun Jim, the bartender, in his Irish Derby, had infectious green eyes, a happy laugh and was always ready with a story for a free drink. Bubba Bill, in his bib overalls was another permanent fixture. The "RK" doubled as a community meeting hall for school plays, Thursday night dance lessons, the Road Kill Triathlon, pack horse races, and on occasion, Karaoke. The Road Kill had its mixture of locals: guest ranch hands, dudes, college students, Forest Service employees, lumberjacks, ranchers, mountain men but very few cowboys, because there were very few cows. Most of them preferred to be called mountain men or women. They wouldn't walk across the street to help a sick cow, but a horse or a mule they would carry out of the mountains on their backs.

▲ ▲ ▲

Shirley drove slowly past the Road Kill remembering the night she first heard Leprechaun Jim tell the Silver Devil story. That night he was holding court and telling of the new drink he had just invented, the Silver Devil.

"Why, Bubba Bill and I had nothing to do that Sunday, so I said let's make up a new drink. Bubba Bill agreed but he said, we had to start with a beer so he could think. So all afternoon we tried gin and vodka, whiskey, tequila mixed with beer, crème de cacao, blueberry brandy, on and on trying every combination we could think of. Along about evening, we were both gettin' a little run down from all this heavy work. I suggested to Bubba Bill that we have a pick me up, our usual shot of good tequila. Bill had just finished trying a shot of crème de menthe and I had a shot of peppermint schnapps. By this time, I wasn't into washing glasses so I just poured the tequila into our shot glasses. We tossed them back. Well that tequila hadn't hit Bubba Bill's tongue a millisecond when he hollered, 'That's the best drink I've ever had.' And I shouted at him, 'You're absolutely wrong. Tequila with just a little bit of this peppermint schnapps is the best drink.'

"Well the shouting went on for about ten minutes before we both realized we weren't going to solve this very serious question. So I said to Bubba Bill, we'll have a contest. Whoever can drink the most of his favorite drink, yours being a shot of tequila with a float of crème de menthe, and mine being a shot of tequila with a float of peppermint schnapps, will earn the right to declare his drink the winner."

"What will we name it," asked Bubba Bill.

"What the devil do I care? It looks like liquid silver to me."

"You're right," he said. "A Silver Devil it is."

This wasn't the first time Bill and I had these kinds of contests so we knew we needed a referee. So we called Easy Lay, who was my backup bartender and only lived five miles away. We took a break to see a man about a horse and just as we were leaving the men's room, Boom! Easy Lay kicked open the door."

"What the hell are the rules and what's in it for me?"

"You get to pour and keep count and then you get to sleep with whoever's still standing," I said.

"Yeah, just like the last time when we ended up out in that old hot springs mudhole asleep when the sun came up and none of us could remember what happened. Hell, I'm ready to go. Let's do it!"

"So Bubba Bill and I began to drink. Now this is a science and those of us who have done this before know that you start out real slow and then pick up the pace. Two, three, four shots go down and on the tenth shot, Bubba Bill stood up and hollered, 'I'm the winner,' because he's so drunk he can't see me. But Easy Lay took Bubba Bill by the hand and showed him I was still there, it's just his eyesight's a little fuzzy. For the rest of the contest, Bill would ask Easy Lay how I was doing. As we passed number fifteen, moving on to number sixteen, our pace had slowed down to where it would take us five minutes to get our hands around the glass just to be sure not to spill. Of course, we both thought in our minds that we were moving at the speed of light, which always happens in one of these contests. At number seventeen Bill's hand just hung in the air about six inches away from his glass. I knew I was closing in for the kill when my hand slowly reached out and encircled number eighteen. Raising number eighteen on high, I shouted, 'I'm the winner. This is the Silver Devil.'

"It took us two days to bring Bubba Bill around. The first day he stayed right at the bar with his hand stuck in the air. The second day he slept on one of the picnic tables outside. I, of course, wasn't affected at all by this contest. However, the back of my head hurt for several days and I just couldn't believe it when Easy Lay said I fell off the back of the stool. That, my fine friends, is how the Silver Devil got its name. I think that calls for another round of drinks. Next Friday I'll tell you the story of Roger Mortis."

This is how a Friday night starts at the Road Kill Café. Storytelling on the porch, a pool table with four players in the middle of the bar, crowded dance floor, band on the stage playing loud music, people four deep at the bar, empty beer bottles on every counter top and ledge, and dogs and kids running between your legs, all on a hot Friday night.

▲ ▲ ▲

Shirley continued her travels and the road got worse and worse. Everyone who has ever driven on that gravel road says that it's terrible. But it is interesting! It changes from June to September. As you leave the pavement, you hit the gravel at a place called Natural Bridge State Park. The gravel at the beginning is very rough because of all the non-experienced drivers who hit the brakes and have rolled up the gravel. So you start your trip at about 10 mph and over the course of the road you reach 25 mph. As you get closer to the ranch, you go back down to 5 mph. Several church camps dot the side of the road as it runs parallel to the Boulder River so you get a glimpse of this gorgeous green-blue river flowing over its boulders and occasional sights of beaver, elk, deer and moose. One time on this road, I counted 250 deer in a five mile stretch. I've also seen mountain lions, bears, foxes and rock chucks.

Traffic is sparse except on weekends when trailers and RVs and 4x4s choke the road. Vehicles pass slowly and carefully trying to avoid breaking their side mirrors from oncoming traffic. Locals use this slowing down as a way to check out the oncoming vehicle and the driver. They also use it as an opportunity to visit with friends and exchange news which often times is faster than the telephone.

You can tell where each vehicle is from by their license plates. The first two digits on a Montana license plate tells you which county the vehicle is registered in, because each county seat has a number. So, if you're from Big Timber (40), your license plate would read maybe 40-1234 and anybody would know you're from Big Timber or thereabouts. If it's 49, you're from Livingston. If it's 3, you are from Billings. People back in the mountains really resent big city people and Billings is the biggest city in Montana with about 85,000 people.

Shirley's next stop as she left the pavement was a place called Natural Bridge. It is a lovely 300 foot waterfall that sprays a rainbow mist into the air when the river is running at flood stage in the spring. It is also the natural formation which divides the upper and lower Boulder river. Shirley stopped, walked the 100 yards to the toilets and all the viewing spots to be sure that everything was clean and proper. Her staff was supposed to have cleaned it early in the morning.

Her next stop was at Aller's Ranch on the Boulder where they had put in speed bumps. She resisted the speed bumps but the Aller's Ranch was on both sides of the road and the people who drove up and down the road went way too fast. The Allers were worried about a serious accident. So she agreed along with the County Superintendent of Roads that they could put in speed bumps which are no more than those concrete pillars they use in parking lots to stop cars. It sure slowed them down. As Shirley drove up she was amazed that it wasn't just but a few weeks ago that the grader had graded the road the whole 22 miles to Box Canyon and now it was just as rough as ever. Of course, all the locals liked that because it helped keep out the tourists. As she moved on up and crossed the Two Mile Bridge by the Double Diamond Ranch, she got out and checked to be sure everything was okay and that nobody was illegally fishing or no animals had gone astray.

Next was Clydehurst Church Camp. Their cook was waving her arms so Shirley pulled over and stopped. "Shirley, Shirley, I'm in trouble!"

"What happened?"

"Well, I came out to unlock the gate and I had the pickup there and I know I took it out of gear, but as soon as I got to the gate, the pickup lurched forward all by itself, blasted through the gate and now it's in the river!"

Shirley could hardly hold back her laughter, but it was funny to see this poor cook out there at 7:30 in the morning, waving her arms while her pickup truck was nose down in the middle of the Boulder River. She said, "Don't worry, I'll get the wrecker out here." So she reached over and called on the CB, "Hey James, this is Shirley up the Boulder at Clydehurst. We've got the cook's pickup in the river. Could you call somebody in town to come out here and tow it out before it washes away?"

"How did it get in the river," asked James.

"She left it in gear when she got out to open the gate."

"Hell, we'll have somebody out there in about an hour."

So the cook said, "What'll I do?"

Shirley says, "Go in and get a cup of coffee. They will be out here in a little bit and they'll pull you out."

She started back up the road, passing a series of beaver dams. Actually everyone says they are beaver dams but Shirley had only seen one once. These beaver dams had been there for thirty years. She stopped and saw several trout swimming through the pond. The water was clear and everything was healthy and she continued on up the road. It was not quite as rough now. She was off the graded part and onto some good old dirt road. This old Chevy truck was going to be okay driving up there. She rounded the bend and drove past a place called Crystal Springs which was once owned by a very famous movie star. The movie star sold it and it was now a struggling new guest lodge. It had three quarters of a mile of the Boulder River on it, and two trout ponds. They were starting to get guests in. She stopped and visited with the manager for a while to see what was going on but she was distracted with the thought of getting up to Yellow Bear Lodge in time to see Wade. She had to figure out a way to get her rope around him, she thought to herself. Everything was fine at Crystal Springs so Shirley continued on.

She flicked on her radio and said, "My ten twenty is at Chippy Park. James, are you on?"

"Yeah, I'm on, Shirley. What's up?"

"Oh, just checking. Hey, why don't you give Wade a call up at Yellow Bear and tell him I'm going to be there in about ten minutes. I want to talk to him about grazing the horses on Forest Service land."

"Will do, Shirley, no problem. Roger and out."

As she came around the bend, she thought back on Chippy Park and smiled to herself as she thought about the history of the valley when there were miners up in Independence. This was the place where the ladies of the night had pitched their tents because it was warmer and didn't snow and they could stay down here longer than they could in Independence which was at 9,500 feet where all the gold mines were. All the locals knew it was a wild gambling whore house business that serviced the miners. She could just see in her mind's eye the low-cut gowns, smiling red lips, hand-on-hips chippies declaring they were open for business. The shouting and laughter filled the air. Now it was just a little park off the side of the road with a couple of camp sites for cars and RVs. Checking the toilets and picking up old beer cans and soda bottles, Shirley smiled at the name and as she stopped, a little camper asked, "Hi, Lady, what's going on? Is this park named after the chipmunks?"

She smiled at the little boy and said, "Yep, we named it Chippy Park after all of the chipmunks that are here." Sometimes it's not good to tell the young ones the real history of places.

As she pulled into Hell's Canyon Campground, she thought about those crazy kayakers that almost got killed the year before. Hell's Canyon is where two mountains come down and meet and the river becomes a two mile waterfall. A series of cascades that drop from 5 to 15 feet with almost no accessibility from the shoreline, the kayakers at high water in May and June think it is great sport to put in at Yellow Bear Lodge and ride the rapids down, coming out at Hell's Canyon Campground. The boy that was taken to the hospital who had cracked his kayak in half hadn't really thought it was much fun riding the whole two miles in a life jacket and just a couple of tennis shoes trying to bounce off the big boulders. He had a slight concussion and a broken rib when they fished him out of the river. Just one of the things Forest Rangers did.

Standing quietly looking at the pond through the trees, Shirley could see a mother moose and her newborn. Standing perfectly still, Shirley knew not to attract the mother's attention.

Tourists don't understand a mother moose is as deadly as a grizzly bear. The moose slowly fed crossing the pond and walked into the trees. The newborn calf on shaky legs was just barely able to make it up the bank after Mom. Shirley walked a few feet and stopped. As the mother came back to check the calf's progress, Shirley said to herself, "Damn, I like my job!"

She turned the corner and crossed onto Yellow Bear Lodge property. She could see the big meadow where the horses were pastured in the summer and she knew that Wade hadn't put the horses in that meadow yet because she could tell by the length of the grass. He had better darn well not have because he didn't have the right to put them in there until June 15th and she was about to come up and give him the mixed good and bad news. As she started on up past their new gate she thought, Hell, looks like Wade got tired of ol' Joe, one of Wade's horses, picking the lock. Here's a big double swinging gate with a lynch pin that goes through the middle of it with two bungee cords plus a large dead bolt lock to hold the gates in place. Of course, I bet it will only take Joe part of the summer to figure out how to undo that. We'll see.

As she drove on up the last quarter mile to the sign that said Guest Entrance, she turned and thought, Oh my God! I thought Wade was going to plow this last piece of driveway. This is the most miserable piece of road on the whole Boulder. He must get some perverse joy out of making his guests drive up a road they wouldn't think their cars could make! So she bumped on up the driveway, around the corner, past some dying thistles. It looked like Wade had been out spraying. I wonder if he's got a permit from us? Damn him. He should have known better than to use 24D without my permission.

As she got up past the entry way, she saw the new construction of the manager's cabin, Wade's residence for the winter. I wonder where the heck Wade is. Man, I hope he asks me out Saturday night to the Road Kill. Boy, just one hour with that man and I could teach him some things he would never, ever, forget. Why the heck doesn't he like me? Well, let me go give him the news. She saw Wade with his shirt off, digging in a trench. She thought she would just slip into the bunkhouse and fix her hair. What's this sign? "Do Not Use the Bathroom." That must be for the guests. Smiling, Shirley sat on the first flush toilet she had seen in a week. Getting up, she flushed, and flushed again. Her hair was fine, no lipstick, just gloss, and she walked out of the bunkhouse toward Wade. He was glistening in the sun, looking very handsome. As she approached, she said, "Hi, Wade! Whatcha digging?"

Smiling back, Wade said, "I was just putting in the last connection on our new septic pipe." Leaning over to attach the right angle, Wade's face turned to a mask of anger, as the freshly flushed toilet deposited its contents on his pants. "Who the hell flushed the toilet? I'll kill them! Shit, shit, shit!"

Trying very hard not to laugh, Shirley said, "You should have put up a Forest Service sign that says, Do not use these facilities by order of the Forest Service." Wade glared, thinking he knew who used the john. Now he would have to wait a day for the trench to dry out.

Getting out of the trench and walking over to the hose, spraying the front of his pants trying to get the worst of it off, he looked at Shirley. "What brings you way up here?"

"Well, it was two things, now I can see, it's three. First the good news. You can put your horses out to pasture three days early. Now the bad news. Your grazing fees are going up two bucks a year. And the third thing is, I'm going to have to issue a citation for having open sewage in a commercial facility."

Wade did not look happy. Holding back his temper, Wade said, "Shirley, you might as well stay for lunch. I'll take a shower and change. Just go up to the lodge and make yourself at home."

Shirley thought to herself, I need to meet Wade's new cook. I hear she's a real knockout.

"Hello? Anyone here? It's Shirley, from the Forest Service."

"Over here," said Marie, "I'm just taking some cookies out of the oven."

She's beautiful, thought Shirley, as she walked up the steps into the kitchen, like an Indian princess. "I'm Shirley."

"I'm Marie. Would you like some coffee?"

"Sure," said Shirley as she turned into the lodge and looked out the windows. "I've never seen the view from here. It's spectacular. What's that on the mountain over there?"

"We call it the howling coyote," Marie said, handing Shirley a mug of coffee. "It was made by a snow avalanche. See his hind legs at the bottom and his head at the top."

"Oh, yes."

"Make yourself at home. Lunch will be ready in fifteen minutes. We serve buffet style," Marie explained. "Guests eat first, then the staff, the manager and me." Shirley looked at the lodge, observing the large pine logs that held up the ceiling and made up the walls. It was very nice. A huge, round, almost walk-in fireplace looked like it could burn a whole tree in a day.

The guests began to drift in. This week wasn't too crowded with about 12 guests total. The talk centered around the morning trailride down to Hell's Canyon and the spectacular view of the river. Some were discussing trout fishing and how many would be caught this afternoon.

"Shirley, what brings you up to the ranch," Marie inquired as she set her plate down, after checking to be sure all the guests had been fed.

Shirley replied, "I had some good and bad news from the Forest Service for Wade." She then related the story of flushing the toilet and why Wade was late for lunch. They both laughed just as Wade came through the door, talking and joking with Ben.

"What are you two lovely ladies laughing about," asked Wade. Marie smiled and got up from the table and went into the kitchen to add some food to the buffet line.

Shirley smiled and said, "It's a girl's joke. I like your shirt. Is it new?"

"Thanks, yes. Got it in Livingston just last week."

"You should save it for the dance Saturday night. You are going, aren't you?"

Wade thought, I sure would like to if Marie's going, "I guess I am. Are you?"

"Sure, why don't we go together? I'm staying at the Four Mile Ranger Station. It would save one of us a trip down the road."

Now I'm stuck, thought Wade. "I'll let you know Friday afternoon if I get that pipe fixed," he smiled, "and no one flushes that toilet again." They went on to discuss the Forest Service grazing permit.

TIPI

One of the spring rituals at the ranch was the "tipi raising." The next morning dawned bright and clear, a good omen. Each year two tipis are erected, one for Wade to live in and the other for guests who wanted a night out in the wilderness. Wade's tipi was set on a little knoll just before the hill fell away steeply down to the road 200 feet below. He had cleared the dead tree branches blocking his line of sight and from the doorway of his tipi he had a view of the trout pond and the river beyond it.

These were authentic Crow Indian tipis, 18 feet in diameter with some added creature comforts that allowed Wade to live in moderate mountain luxury. He had added wall-to-wall carpeting, electricity, a queen size bed, a refrigerator, heater, a closet pole hung between two tipi poles, a port-a-potty and hat hangers made out of leather thongs with a short stick at the end. These hat hangers were hung from the lodgepoles in convenient locations around the tipi. In addition, Wade had attached banners to the main lodgepole outside and hung an old wig that gave the impression of scalps. He made up a great story for the guests.

Now Wade was a handsome man, but he did suffer from some hair loss. A circular patch of bare scalp on the back of his head was usually covered up by his cowboy hat. But Wade knew that looks were only skin deep and he used this as a wonderful opportunity to spread some tall tales among the younger guests. On Sunday evenings after dinner it was his custom to volunteer to lead a tour of the ranch for the new guests that had checked in that afternoon. He especially encouraged the kids to come with him so he could point out all the really good places to play hide and seek in the trees or go climbing on the rocks. Every tour included a stop by Wade's tipi where he would give a talk called "How My Scalp Came To Be Hanging From My Tipi."

He would gather them outside the tipi describing how the animal designs had been chosen, and that the red war shields with the yellow feathers painted all around the entrance indicated this was a chief's tipi and therefore belonged to him. Then he would pause dramatically and point up at the banners and the hank of long black hair tied to the top of the lodgepole and ask, "Can you see that scalp up there blowing in the wind? That's a real human scalp. In fact, that's my scalp!" And he would sweep off his hat and bend over so everyone could see his bald spot and he would explain.

"Back in 1887 I got into a fight with an angry Crow Indian Warrior over a lovely Indian maiden. We went at it tooth and nail, but he got the better of me that day and he scalped me. With one big slice of his big Bowie knife, swoosh, my hair and half my scalp were in his hands. I wore my hair longer in those days and I had a long ponytail. Anyway, he was going to leave me to rot, but I talked him out of it. In fact, it took me three days but I finally talked him into giving me back my scalp. Well, a scalp is big medicine, even if it is your own, so I hung it at the top of that lodgepole to watch over my home. And that's how my scalp came to be hanging from my tipi!"

The poles for the tipi had been oiled the previous fall and set standing up leaning against the other trees for support. They stayed that way until spring. Wade, Ben and Cindy began by placing four poles on the ground. The Crows used four poles, while other tribes used three. As Wade finished lashing the four poles together at the top, he said, "Cindy, you grab that tie down rope and pull while Ben and I lift. Okay, pull. Ben, you lift up those two over there. Up, up, okay stop. Spread those two, and now these two. We have to get all four of these poles set in the right directions. Southeast, southwest, northeast, northwest, because the entrance must always face east. The entrance poles are the last ones we'll set up."

"Why east," asked Cindy.

"The Plains Indians were very smart. They knew that the winds generally came out of the west or south and the sun rising in the east in the morning would shine into the doorway and warm up the interior. The afternoon sun, when it was hot, would hit the back of the tipi.

"Gee, I guess they were smart," said Cindy.

"Now that we've got these four up, Cindy and Ben, bring over the other poles one at a time and we'll set them up one at a time, in order. Two squaws could put up a tipi in about a half hour. It's taking the three of us half a day. We're sure not very good Indians." Ben chuckled. The Indians didn't have to add carpeting, electricity and a queen size bed.

Things went quickly after that. The outer canvas was attached to the lifting pole and all three of them together lifted it into position and spread out the canvas. Wade climbed the ladder to affix the willow fasteners and Cindy held down the center tie down rope. Wade had learned after sleeping in the tipi for a few years, that the Sioux were smarter than the Crow because they wrapped the tie down rope around the poles at the top to keep them from rattling in the wind. "Wade, where do I tie this rope down," Cindy asked.

"To the south side against the wind inside the tipi," Wade explained. "That gives me more room inside and the strongest support against the wind so that this tipi doesn't turn into a kite."

"Wade, are you going to have a tipi raising ceremony," asked Ben.

"Sure, we'll do both tomorrow night, after we set up the guest tipi. Give me a hand with this bed, will you?"

"Ain't you going over board with a refrigerator, heater and queen size bed and all this other stuff?"

"Ben, I live here from June to October. It's my home. Your tent has just as much stuff."

"I ain't got no refrigerator."

"But you have one in the bunkhouse. Now the two of you help me with this liner, will you?"

"What's it for," asked Cindy.

"It keeps it cool inside in the summer, by catching the air at the bottom outside and guiding the hot air inside up and out the hole at the top. It's a built-in Indian air-conditioner. Plus it forces all the flies and bugs out the top and acts as a shield to keep people from seeing shadows when it's lit at night. And remember, " Wade said laughingly, "The rules are, when the tipi's rocking, don't come knocking."

▲ ▲ ▲

"Pam, are you going to the tipi ceremony tonight? What's it like," asked Leigh. Leigh, a 20 year old blond with braces was a freshman at Montana State University and had been hired by Anna Wilson, along with Pam. Their job was to clean the rooms and cabins in the mornings after doing the dishes in the kitchen after meals. They usually had afternoons off and were done with dinner dishes by 8:00 pm. Pam had a different idea about her job. This was her second year at the ranch and as a beautiful, long legged brunette, and an experienced young lady of 22, she saw her job as one of training Leigh in the ways of men first, getting herself laid second, partying third, and working a distant fourth.

They were in the kitchen mopping the floor, the last chore of the night. Leigh was rinsing out the mop and bucket. "Leigh, what, are you crazy? You don't have to do that. We're going to the RK. I haven't been laid since Thursday. Besides, don't you want to practice getting laid with a full bladder to see if the orgasm is more intense," exclaimed Pam.

"Pam," Leigh shouted. "I've never had an orgasm! Don't you remember what I asked you at the campfire the other night after everyone was gone?"

"No, I don't. I must have had too much beer," said Pam.

"I asked you how do you tell when a man comes, and you just laughed. And I still need an answer."

Pam laughed, "Leigh, it's going to be a fun summer teaching you about sex, mountain men and partying. Now get dressed and put on some makeup because we're going to hit the RK for some heavy partying."

As Leigh was getting dressed, Pam continued Leigh's education in partying by explaining that the best way was not to drive to the Road Kill, but to get the guys to come to the ranch, bring their own booze and stay over. That way, you had the best of both worlds. Free booze, little or no competition for the guys and you didn't have to worry about driving home from the Road Kill.

"Sometimes we get lucky and get the right mix of guests so that we don't have to invite any of the local guys. My rule is that if he's male and over sixteen, he's fair game. It's so much fun teaching those young boys what a real woman is like. Last year we had this eighteen year old that had never done it. One night Crazy Jane and I took him to the guest tipi. Crazy Jane gave him his first blow job and I was his first lay. He stayed hard for hours. I think we each did him about ten times that week. He went away a very happy camper! Now hurry up, it's almost 8:00 pm."

"When will we get back," asked Leigh.

"When the sun comes up. We don't have to be back at work until 7:30 am. No problem!"

▲ ▲ ▲

Wade was standing in the buffet line for dinner in his usual place, last in line, except for the cook. It was ranch policy that the guests eat first, then the staff, manager and lastly, the cook. Wade joked with the guests that they should hurry through the line because the staff was always hungry and they carried knives. There were good reasons for this. The cook learned how much people like to eat and would prepare the correct proportions. Marie and Wade were in constant conflict. Wade wanted to be sure there was plenty of food for the guests and staff and Marie wanted to have just enough so that she minimized food costs and didn't have large amounts of leftovers to deal with.

Wade's eyes fixed on the tuna noodle casserole that was dwindling rapidly. He said jokingly to Marie, "Your tuna noodle casserole looks great," as a guest stepped in front of him and took the last piece on the serving dish.

Marie stepped up, removed the serving dish with a smile. "Wade, I'm sorry. It looks like we're out. Would you like a peanut butter and jelly sandwich instead," she asked with a twinkle in her eye. Wade looked crestfallen and walked into the kitchen with Marie right behind him.

In his best manager's voice he said, "Marie, we need to talk about food and quantities again," as he took the jar of peanut butter off the shelf.

"Why," Marie asked. Just then Ben came to the window and stuck his head in.

"Any more casserole Marie?"

"Sure, for you, Ben," she said as she turned gracefully, removing a serving dish from the oven. "I was holding some back for the staff." Wade grinned. He knew when he had been tricked.

He laughed and said, "I'll think I'll have some peanut butter and humble pie on top of my casserole." All the guests laughed at that one. They had all taken heaping plates of casserole so Wade would end up short. Tricking the boss was great sport for all.

Cindy waved Wade over and patted the empty seat next to her. "Gotcha! Didn't we," said Cindy.

"Yes, that Marie is some prankster. But I'll get even. It's a long summer."

"Wade, I've got a line on three new horses. I heard from a friend near Three Forks. Are we interested," asked Cindy

ROGER MORTIS

The story of Roger Mortis has been told for years and years on the front steps of the Road Kill Café. Noble Tweedy was a grand story teller. This afternoon as Wade pulled up in his truck to pick up the groceries from Sysco, Tweedy was telling his story to any tourist that would listen and buy him a beer, about Roger Mortis, the blond grizzly bear that had been skinned right there at the Road Kill.

"Roger," began Noble, "was a young bear, maybe two or three years old when he first found out about the Road Kill. His nose led him down off the mountain, right up here on the porch. That bear could smell liqueurs a mile away. This particular night he managed to jam his paw under the outside window right here. Even though he weighed about three hundred pounds, he managed to slide through the window and get himself into the bar. There he started to try out every berry liqueur he could find. He had peach brandy, blackberry brandy, huckleberry brandy, blueberry and apricot brandy and just about any other sweet liqueur you could think of. He made quite a mess and as you might guess, they found him sound asleep on the porch on the picnic table. Now Leprechaun Jim, the manager and bartender, had a pretty big heart when he saw this poor bear and knew what kind of a hangover he was going to have. So he didn't shoot him, but tied a rope to him, hooked it on to his trailer hitch and drug him across the road into the big field that led up to the big mountains. Jim came back to the bar that day and thought to himself, I'll let him get away with it once, but if he ever comes back, he's one dead bear. That yellow hide would make a nice trophy on my wall when he gets about six hundred pounds or so.

Roger suffered from a hangover that would have killed a human being. He spent most of the next week soaking in a high Alpine lake until his eyes started to focus again.

Several years passed before Roger started to notice girl bears. By this time he was almost six hundred pounds. He first laid eyes on Riga," Tweedy continued, "when he was about five years old. For Roger, it was bear love at first sight and after a whirlwind courtship of rolling rocks, tearing up old wooden logs, and sharing the remains of an elk kill, Riga agreed to be his mate. Now in bear culture, the male bear takes the female bear's last name. So Roger became Roger Mortis, and of course, Riga, was his new wife.

"During their courtship, Roger had explained to Riga about the wonderful time he had at the Road Kill Café and the number of berry flavored liquids you could drink there. They made you feel really great, then you fell asleep and you woke up somewhere else. If you had an Alpine lake close by, the after effects weren't so bad."

Tweedy looked off toward the distant range of mountains, finished his beer and smiled, handing the empty to the nearest tourist. "I'm a bit dry. Is there a chance I can get another?"

Wade looked at him and thought, Tweedy will stretch this story out all afternoon until one or another thing happens. Either the bar runs out of beer or the tourist has to leave. Not much of a chance of either of those two things happening since there's a steady supply of both coming through the door.

Cold beer arrived. Tweedy snatched it out of the air and said, "Where was I? Oh, yes, Roger was bragging to Riga about this place where all the berry liquids were. Riga agreed that it must be just great, and maybe they could find it again on their wedding night. Roger thought that was a great idea and he set his nose to sniffing the air. Within several days, he caught a whiff of liqueurs which in fact was nothing more than stale beer, but then again, his nose wasn't well trained. So on a full moonlit night, about three in the morning, Roger and Riga sauntered over the ridge and down the mountain right up to this very spot where we're sitting. Roger tried his old trick of lifting up the window, but he'd forgotten he was twice as big as before, so he had to find a different way to get in. Letting his nose lead the way, he found his way around to the side door. Like all bears who want something, he stood up on his hind legs and pushed all his six hundred pounds against that flimsy door. With a creak and a groan, it shattered. Roger bearwalked his way in, across the dance floor and up to the bar. Riga, being a little more cautious because there were lots of human smells around, took her time and checked out all the corners. Roger being an old hand at this, turned and said to Riga, 'You might like the apricot brandy best, but I prefer the huckleberry.' He proceeded to knock bottles down to the floor and the party was on. There were bears whooping and dancing, and licking and growling, having a good old time until both bears decided to take a nap about six am. Roger cuddled Riga in his paws and they fell asleep on the barroom stage."

Tweedy paused, sipping his beer and gathering his thoughts. "Now you know," looking the tourist straight in the eye, "Most Montana stories don't have happy endings. Leprechaun

Jim arrived at the bar at his usual time and opened the front door. He was almost knocked over by the smell of stale booze and bear piss. One quick glance told him that his old friend, Roger, had come back to try his old liqueur trick again. He slipped out and got his 30.06 rifle out of the truck. Peering carefully through the door, he realized he had a very dangerous situation on his hands. It would be two drunk grizzly bears or two hung over grizzly bears and he couldn't make up his mind which would be worse. He also realized he couldn't shoot them in the bar because that would make a worse mess and he wouldn't be able to open today. Since it had worked before when the bear was smaller, he thought he could rope one of the bears, pull it out of the bar with his truck and maybe the other bear wouldn't wake up. He went out, backed his pickup up to the door, hooked his lariat to the trailer hitch and slowly stepped inside. Both bears were sleeping peacefully. The closest bear to him happened to be Riga. He flipped the lariat around her shoulders, tightened the loop and jumped into the pickup. Slowly he began to drag her out the door, down these very steps, across the gravel and out into the field you see over there. She didn't even wake up. So he went back for Roger. Just as he fashioned the loop around Roger's head, Roger began to wake. Jim ran quickly to the truck, threw it in gear and started the truck. As Roger was dragged across the floor, a piece of glass slit him from his chin to his tail and all that Jim got as it came out the door, was a grizzly bear hide. What remained of Roger went out the back door and hightailed it east. That's how Leprechaun Jim got himself that gorgeous yellow bear hide hanging on the wall in there without firing a shot. The moral of this story is, if you hang around those bars drinking all that sweet stuff, you're gonna wake up one morning with your hide gone."

The tourist laughed, bought Noble Tweedy another beer and moved on. Wade sat down and said, "Noble, why don't you ever tell the true story about how Yellow Bear Valley got its name?"

"Oh, I'll do that next week, when we got a new bunch of Cheechakos (tenderfeet)."

MOUNTAIN LION

Later that month Cindy and Jake were down at the corral. "Cindy, we got six signed up for the ride."

"Yeah, I checked them out this morning at breakfast. That one guy is big, maybe two hundred twenty or two hundred thirty pounds. Put him on Dixie. Put the two kids on Julie and Jahaa and the rest you can choose. Who are you riding today?"

"Blackie. He needs the work."

The ride went out without a hitch, Jake in the lead, Cindy riding drag. "Hey, Jake! Let's try that new trail over on the other side of the river." Jake and Cindy had cleared the trail two days before. It offered the guests a chance to cross the river twice, plus a beautiful view of the valley and the river. Cindy loved it, but Jake had spotted mountain lion tracks while he was chopping a tree that had fallen across the trail. He told Cindy that they might be close to a mountain lion den and if there were cubs present, it would be very dangerous to ride through the area. Cindy said that wasn't a problem because she was carrying her .44 Smith and Wesson. Besides, the horses would tell them way in advance if the lion was around. "We should wait a week or so before we use that trail," Jake said over his shoulder.

"It's okay," Cindy said with a smile.

She's the boss, thought Jake, as he led the group down the gravel bank into the river. Riding a horse across this beautiful crystal clear river was always a thrill. You could look down and see the rocks on the bottom and watch the fish flash behind boulders as the horses carefully picked their way across. Jake thought to himself, I should bring a fly rod and fish from the back of a horse. That way I wouldn't get my feet wet. But what if I caught something? How would I release it?

Jake rode up out of the river looking back to check the guests. Everything was fine. Just then he saw a movement out of the corner of his eye. A coyote looked up at the riders then down at the ground. It had a mouse or a mole trapped. Jake didn't say a word because he didn't want to spook the coyote. He just pointed so the guests could look as they passed. Coyotes weren't a problem. There were five or six of them around the ranch off and on all summer. Their evening serenades to the moon added an extra touch of entertainment for the guests. It was that mountain lion he was worried about. Riding lead he could always spot the signs first. He hadn't gone 200 yards before, "Oh shit! There were new claw marks on that tree that weren't there two days ago. It's a cat all right. Too small for bear marks. Looks like the mountain lion is marking his territory." Off to the left, were trees with the bark rubbed off by the elk and deer trying to get the velvet off their antlers. Shit, cat tracks in the mud with one, no, two kitten prints, Jake thought.

Jake's head began to rotate slowly side to side watching for movement. His hand rested on the stock of the .30-30 rifle in the scabbard on his saddle. His horse, Blackie, seemed to sense the danger too. Jake was checking Blackie's ears and as they rounded the rock avalanche with boulders as big as houses, Jake spotted the lion above them about 100 yards to the right. So did Blackie. He stopped and started to turn back. Jake knew that would be fatal, so he kicked Blackie and started forward, slowly. This time he didn't point. It would be better if the guests didn't know what danger they were in.

Slowly, the eight horses and riders passed under the lion. The lion didn't blink. It's tail flicked from side to side. Cindy had seen Jake and Blackie's reaction and had quickly spotted the lion. She placed her hand on the .44 and rode slowly ahead. The guests passed by one by one. To Cindy it seemed an eternity. As they made the turn back towards the river, Cindy looked back to check on the mountain lion. It had moved down to the trail without making a sound. It just sat there watching the horses and riders disappear around the bend. I sure don't want to be on this trail after dark, Cindy thought. They rode back over the river up through the trees and slowly walked up to the corral.

"Great ride. Wished we had seen more wildlife. Maybe tomorrow," one of the guests said.

"Yep," said Jake as he looked up at Cindy and slowly shook his head. After the guests left, Cindy sat on the corral fence.

"Jake, you handled that just right. We sure didn't need a guest having a wreck while mother mountain lion was watching."

"Yessum."

"We'll take that ride off the list for a week or so."

"Yessum."

Cindy looked at Jake and thought, he never looks up, just says, "Yessum," with his hat covering his eyes. I wonder what he's hiding. A broken heart or something else?

Jake took a scoop of horse cookies and tossed them out into the corral. This job was like flying one of them aeroplanes. Hours and hours of boredom followed by 30 seconds of sheer terror. "Blackie, you did great today. Let me check that shoe," he said, as he gently put his hand on the front of Blackie's leg.

"Jake, I'll see you at the lodge for lunch," Cindy said as she started the quarter mile walk up to the lodge. Jake was left to his own thoughts. Maybe this afternoon, after the ride, I'll take Apache fishing. Apache loves the water. Every time he goes to the pond for a drink, he wades in up to his belly.

WILD WOMEN'S NIGHT OUT

Sitting around the campfire after all the guests had gone to bed, Anna began to explain to Marie and Cindy about the Yellow Bear Lodge tradition of "Wild Women's Night Out." Leaning forward and lowering her voice, Anna said, "Each year, the mature women on the ranch gather in a hidden location around nine o'clock in the evening."

"By mature, I presume you mean all the gals that aren't screwing every pair of pants that walks onto this ranch," Cindy asked.

"Yes," laughed Anna. "The ones that have a little more spiritual side to their natures. But we have to prepare. A large stock of supplies has to be laid in. Firewood, paper, booze, food, poems, stories, blankets and a cigar or two will be needed. Three years ago we all went down to the river and went skinny dipping. A very sobering experience in forty-eight degree water. But here's my proposal for this year. Cindy, you scout a location along the river that's secluded so that a campfire can't be seen from anywhere else. Marie, you supply the food. We'll all chip in for the booze and I'll bring some stories and some raunchy poetry."

"Let's pick a night when the cabin girls have gone to the Road Kill," Marie said.

Cindy laughed. "That's almost every night of the week. I've got just the spot. There's a big flat rock hidden between two large boulders right on the bank of the river in the middle of the Cascades where the river runs over the rock slide. It's perfect."

"Looks like the only night we can do it would be Wednesday. Tuesday and Friday are cookouts and Thursday is dancing at the Road Kill. Wednesday is the only day one of us isn't off," volunteered Anna.

"Okay, let's do it," Marie said and they all clasped hands to make a pact.

The next few days were especially fun for the three women. Having a shared secret always was. They quietly assembled their supplies. Cindy found a spot not far from the swimming hole. It was sandy and surrounded by big boulders so flames from a fire would be blocked. In her spare time she collected firewood and kindling.

Marie baked a special batch of cookie bars filled with chopped almonds, coconut and frosted with chocolate and saved a dozen for the event. A couple of apples, some cheese, some hard peppermint candy, the cookies and a thermos of brandy laced coffee should do the trick, she thought.

Anna found her copy of Robert Service's poems and a couple of special poems she had collected over the years. In the back of her closet she had a supply of colorful scarves they could tie in a dozen ways.

Wednesday night arrived. After dinner, each of them made up an excuse and withdrew from the easy banter going on in the lodge with the guests. They met outside the bunkhouse, coats and blankets in hand and Cindy led the way. The twilight would last another hour and as the three of them walked single file down the path past the trout pond toward the river, their spirits soared. Each was looking forward to sharing stories and building the bonds of friendship and womanhood. There is something special about campfires in the dark under a black and twinkling sky with the comforting embrace of the mountains all around.

They arrived at the rock in silence, but as they put down their things and made themselves comfortable they fell into easy conversation. "Here, you guys. Nothing jump starts a party like costumes. Take two," Anna said as she passed around the colorful silks. Marie chose a red and purple scarf that she tied around her head like an Indian headband. Another one she tied around her waist. Cindy chose a black and white scarf she tied around her neck. Anna chose a dark green print scarf for headband and a yellow and white one for around her waist. Marie opened the thermos and passed around the hot coffee laced with brandy in Styrofoam cups.

"So, Cindy, how's life treating you? How are you settling in at the ranch," asked Anna.

"Gosh, just fine, I guess. The horses are great and Wade is great to work for," Cindy replied. "I worry about Jake though. He's so darn shy. Won't look you in the eye to save his life!"

"Something happened to that boy that traumatized him," Anna theorized, "And not too long ago either! Marie, why don't you break out the cookies you made. I haven't been able to think of very much else since I smelled them baking the other day. Give him some time Cindy, and he'll come out of it."

"What about you, Anna? How did you come to work at the ranch," Marie asked. "You've been here longer than anyone."

"Oh, Lord. It's been so long I can't hardly remember. Seems like forever that I've been packing Sam off to the woods for the summer and then turning around and coming up here," Anna said.

"But don't you miss him terribly," Marie asked.

"When you've been married as long as we have, it seems more like a vacation than anything else. If nothing else, I get a break from his snoring," hooted Anna. The girls all laughed and Anna took a big sip of coffee.

"Okay, Marie. Tell us some more about yourself," prodded Anna.

"There's nothing much to tell. I've been married more times than I care to admit and I just got divorced again from the biggest mistake I ever made. You would think I would learn," Marie confessed. "I'm determined not to make another one. I just want to have a smooth, problem free life," she added.

"There ain't no such thing," Anna said. "If there were we never would get wrinkles and gray hair. You gotta take life by the horns," she insisted. "Besides, I've noticed there's a funny way you and Wade look at each other," Anna said.

"I'm not leading him on, Anna. He's just being nice like he is to everyone else," Marie said.

"There's nice and then there's I-can-hardly-keep-my-hands-off-you nice. But it's none of my business. Say, there's a great poem I want to read you guys. It's called "The Ballad of the Ice Worm Cocktail." Then we can get started on the ghost stories. Cindy, you must know a bunch of them, you've spent so much time outdoors. Let's refill the coffee cups and I'll get started. Let's see now, I think it's on page 79," and Anna was off to educate and entertain a new crew of co-workers that would be depending on each other for support and comfort in the coming months. The night would dwindle slowly and they would get silly and get to know each other a little better before they called it quits for the night and snuck back to their bunks on the ranch. Each would feel the bonds of friendship grow stronger after tonight's passing.

FLYFIJHING

Wade and his flyfishing guest had been on the river for about an hour. The guest had caught and released five fish and Wade had just changed his fly to a Joe's Hopper.

"The fish will be stacked on each side of that boulder waiting for the hopper to drift around to the side. Put your fly just in front of that boulder, give it lots of line and just let it drift," Wade explained.

Following his directions, the guest tried several casts. "Not so much arm. It's in the wrist. Watch the wind. Keep it to your back," he said.

The sun reflected off the water and the wind sent little riffles across the surface. Wade looked out across the river and over the thousands of pine trees thinking that his must be the most beautiful spot on earth. What a great way to make a living. Wade could see the fish in the cold, crystal clear water. They were stacked one on top of the other on the near side of the rock. The guest's fly finally landed in front of the rock and the current began to drag it around the side.

"Wow, I've got one," the guest exclaimed, "I've got one!"

"Easy, easy," Wade said. "I'll help you release it." Wetting his hands, Wade slowly moved his hand down the line to the leader. "It's a beautiful Cutthroat, about twelve inches long. Look at the red and orange colors under his gills. They run all the way down his belly." Wade gently pulled the barbless hook from the fish's mouth. Releasing his hands from around the fish, he pointed it up stream, so the trout's gills would fill. The fish flashed away then turned back to brush against Wade's leg. This often happened. He didn't know if this was because the fish was confused or just a way of thanking him for being set free.

A large splash was followed by, "Whoa, whoa. Hold still you damn horse!" Wade jerked his head up and looked upstream. The sight he saw made him burst into laughter. There was Jake on Apache, the brown and white paint, bucking down the middle of the river reins in one hand, fly rod in the other with a 10" or 12" fish on the end.

"I guess Jake hasn't worked all the kinks out of flyfishing from horseback," Wade explained to the guest. Just then, Jake lost his seat and landed on his back in a big pool. Wade shouted, "Jake, did you lose the fish?" Jake stood up shaking the water off his hat and pulling it back down over his eyes.
"Nope, still got him." Fly pole in one hand, the other holding up his wet pants, Jake splashed to the bank where Apache stood looking at him with that look like, "How stupid is this guy?"

Wade laughed. "Jake's been talking for weeks about fishing from horseback so he could keep his feet dry. Looks like he just got his first lesson."

JAKE AND THE GIRLS

Jake was the picture of relaxation. Feet up by the fire, hat over his eyes, beer in his right hand, he was just about to drop off to sleep. It had been another 14 hour day. Wade had walked the guests up from the campfire and even Cindy had gone up to the bunkhouse early leaving just Jake, Pam and Leigh. Pam and Leigh were giggling and slurping their beer.

Poor Jake didn't know he was the reason behind the giggles and the reason Pam and Leigh had stayed behind at the campfire. Earlier that day over washing pots and pans when no one was around to hear them, Pam had suggested they get Jake into Leigh's room in the bunkhouse and both "share him" together.

Leigh wasn't sure. "You see, Pam. I've only done it twice, once at school and once at the RK, and well," she sighed, "three people together, I would feel weird."

"Leigh, grow up. I'll get him all heated up and then I'll leave and you can take over. You can even go over to his tent, although I like mattresses better than wooden floors," Pam said.

Beers in hand, Pam and Leigh sat down on either side of Jake. He grunted in surprise. "Jake, I've got some pictures developed from rodeo weekend. Why don't you come up to my room and Leigh and I will show them to you," Pam said, as she leaned close and brushed her breasts against his arm.

Leigh put her hand on the inside of his thigh. "Please," she said softly. "Please. I have a cold six-pack of beer I'll share," Leigh whispered.

"Trapped," flashed through Jake's mind. "Tomorrow," he said.

"No, no, tonight," Pam whispered as she pressed her breast harder against his arm.

Leigh's hand moved closer to his crotch. Swiftly jumping up Jake said, "Sorry ladies, I have to see a man about a horse," as he swiftly moved off toward the bunkhouse bathroom.
"Pam, we've lost him," Leigh said.

"No we haven't. Follow me." Arriving at the door to Leigh's room just down the hall from the bunkhouse bathroom, Pam pushed Leigh through the doorway. "Take off all your clothes, hurry, and put on this robe. I'll stop Jake as he comes down the hall and you can flash him. That should get his attention."

Soon Jake stepped out of the bathroom and spotted Pam standing in the archway of Leigh's door. "Trapped again," flashed through his mind.

"Jake, come here!" Pam commanded. Jake moved slowly down the hall, head down, hat covering his eyes. "I've got something better to show you than rodeo pictures," Pam said as she pushed the door open further. Jake looked up and there stood Leigh with her robe held open by her hands on her hips in her panties and bra.

"Well, do you like what you see?" Leigh asked with a nervous giggle.

"Yessum," Jake replied.

"Come in then," Pam said giving him a push.

"I, I," he stammered, "think I should go to my tent to get a few things."

"We have all the condoms you need right here," Pam said.

Knowing actions were better than words, Jake ducked under Pam's arm into the hallway and out the door before either Pam or Leigh could move. Walking quickly to his tent, he grabbed his sleeping bag and pillow and headed to the corral. "It'll be safer sleeping with the horses, mountain lions or grizzly, rather than those two polecats," he thought.

"So now what do we do." Leigh asked.

"We go to his tent, and do it there," Pam replied. "But first, we prepare. I'll be back."

Throwing the flap of the tent open they yelled, "Surprise!" Pam and Leigh backlit by the yard light were standing at the entrance to the tent wearing open robes and bikinis.

"Now what?"

"I guess he's not in the mood," sighed Pam. "We might as well go to bed."

SUNBATHING

At last, an afternoon off, Wade though to himself as he ducked, stepping out of the tipi. Dressed in his shorts that doubled as a swimming suit, fly pole and fishing vest in hand, he was headed off to his favorite fishing and sunbathing spot in Hell's Canyon. It was about a mile down the river from the ranch's favorite swimming hole where the rest of the staff normally spent their afternoons playing in the waterfalls.

Wade had found this spot while fishing with a guest. A large flat rock in the middle of the river was hidden around a bend with large Douglas Fir trees sheltering it from the wind. He would fish until the fish got wise and then lie back in the corner of the rock and soak up the sun. It was a time to be alone, far away from ranch problems and a time to think about his future.

Wade's stride lengthened as he thought of that lovely spot and all the golden cutthroat waiting for him. Ducking under the limb of a fir tree, he saw someone lying on his rock. Long black hair, skin glowing in the sun from sweat and suntan lotion, Marie had found his secret spot. No! She couldn't be here. She was supposed to be upstream with the rest of the girls. He took several soft steps closer but stopped suddenly when he realized she wasn't wearing a top to her swim suit. Her breasts were firm and the large beautiful nipples were erect from the cool breeze. He leaned forward to get a closer look when "snap," a branch broke underneath his foot. It sounded like a rifle shot. Marie's head jerked up, she grabbed her towel and shouted, "Who's there?"

Wade turned to leave but stopped because he knew if he left she would be frightened, so he moved forward to the edge of the tree line where the water began. "Hi, it's me. What are you doing at my favorite fishing hole?"

"I don't see your name on it," she said with a slow smile. Hunching down on his heels, and as seriously as he could, Wade said, "We're not allowed to write on the rocks and trees by order of the Forest Service." Picking up a flat stone, he skipped it across the river making little splashes until the final one splashed three icy drops of water on Marie. Why aren't you up with the other girls by the waterfall?"

Marie thought. Should I tell him the truth or should I just say I wanted to be alone and found this perfect spot where no one would find me?

"Well, I'll leave you to it," Wade said, as he turned to walk back through the trees.

"No," Marie said. "Two can share this rock. Let me put my top on and then you can swim out." The swim to the rock was always refreshing even if it took his breath away. Marie stuck out her hand and pulled him up onto the rock as droplets of cold water dripped across her chest, making her nipples spring to life again. Wade sat down on his towel next to hers and stretched out in the clear, warm sun. Their legs brushed and the electric shock he felt during the interview when he first touched her, sent sparks to the other reaches of his body. His manhood was quickly recovering from the river's icy effects. Marie turned so she could look at his chest and slowly reached out to touch the shiny, wet black hairs with the palm of her hand A butterfly landed on his shoulder and she thought about the poem she had written.

Once in a while, a strong hand and a butterfly may touch
And love so much.
That spark of love, the taste of love, is like the touch of a butterfly.
Once you've brushed the touch, your body, mind and soul
Can never say goodbye.

The butterfly flew off into the bright sun. Sensing that she was suddenly receptive, Wade leaned over and kissed her on the forehead. She turned her lips up, looked into his eyes, curled an arm around his neck and kissed him with her whole body, mind and soul. Breaking away slowly from that lovely kiss, Marie stood up taking her towel in her hand and wading through the shallow water on the other side, led Wade to the far bank where the soft moss and sand made a wonderful bed.

Making love at the side of the river in the sunshine left their bodies spent from the exhilaration but longing for more. Wade could not touch her enough. His hand roamed her body, exploring all her private places again and again. He needed her one more time, but this time, much more slowly. Marie responded to each caress, needing him to continue on and on until there was nothing but the sky, the river and the trembling in her loins that burst into stars over her whole being. Just as he thrust forward, he raised his head and moaned, "Awww, oh, oh, oh!"

They rested quietly in the afterglow of their lovemaking holding each other as spoons. "Marie, are you happy?"

"Oh yes! That was wonderful. Let's do that again!"

"You are too much for me, young lady."

"No, I'm not," as she took him in her hand. He instantly came to life again. "But I have to go to work, or you won't get any dinner and your guests will complain. Maybe I can stop by your tipi later tonight?" She got up, put on her suit and slipped into the frigid water. She threw him a kiss as she struck out for the far shore

Wade lay there wondering what had hit him. It was so wonderful. Better than any other time in his life. It just felt so good, the glow of it. No other woman had made him feel that way. Leaning back against the shore, he thought, this was a lot better than flyfishing!

Later as the campfire was dying down and the guests were slowly drifting off to their cabins, Wade made his way toward his tipi that sat on the ridge overlooking the river. Minutes later there was a scratching on his door.

"Wade, can I come in?"

"Sure, Marie. Let me get the tie down loose."

She stepped through the door, standing up straight in her Indian dress. Reaching up first to her left shoulder and than her right, she unbuckled the clasps and her dress dropped to the floor, leaving her naked.

"God, you're beautiful!"

"So are you," she said as she moved into his arms. "Life is wonderful."

Days drifted into weeks as Marie and Wade's affair blended into the life of the ranch. The float trip went out almost every week under Ben Johnson's watchful eye and the 4x4 trip was always exciting.

"Ben, how was the trip today," Wade asked.

"Great, just one small problem. You know that big grizzly bear that has been bothering the sheep herders. Well, he's taken up residence on Monument Peak and I don't think we'll be taking any more hikes up there for a while," Ben said.

"You're right, Ben. Just let them have their space. We're in their country. Let's see if we can get some water down to the campfire. I'm very worried about starting a wildfire. Let's go over and look at that old valve I found." Wade turned the valve on.

"Look," Ben exclaimed. "There's water coming out of a pipe by the bunkhouse. We can make a connection there right down to the fire pit."

"Ben, I'm not sure about this. We don't know where this water goes to. I sure wish the owner had made a schematic of the water and power. But let's give it a try."

Later that day after they had connected a water pipe and run a hose to the campfire, Ben started the cooking fire for Marie. He felt a lot better about the reduced chance of a wildfire. The cook's helpers arrived about 5:30 to begin setting up dinner. Ben helped with the grill that covered about one half of the fire pit. This being the first cookout of the year, everyone was on a high learning curve. The cook's helpers forgot the paper plates and Pam was sent back to the lodge for them. Ben shouted, "Don't forget the PAM for the grill," smiling at his pun. Overall, everyone was happy. The guests were trying to rope the wooden cow named Norman. Some were playing horseshoes. Cindy Tucker, the head wrangler, was leading demonstrations in roping and flirting with all the males over sixteen. It was a beautiful, quiet evening. The fire was crackling. A lone crow flew over the cookout when Ben's head jerked up. He picked up some movement out of the corner of his eye. His mountain man instincts came sharply into focus.

"Wade, mind if I add a little variety to this here cookout?" Wade smiled and Ben moved quickly and quietly to the bunkhouse. Retrieving his .22 rifle he quickly stalked a rough grouse. In less than five minutes he was laying two freshly cleaned grouse breasts on the grill. Some guests and the new hired help, Pam and Leigh, were a little shocked after learning

Ben had just stalked, shot, cleaned and cooked his own dinner in less than 10 minutes. As Ben sliced the breasts and handed out samples, you could hear little murmurs, "Wow, is this good! Is there any more?"

Wade smiled. I guess I don't have to worry about his skills as a guide this fall, he thought to himself.

Jerome, a guest from California asked Wade, "What's on the agenda for tonight?

Wade replied, "Volleyball and after dinner if it's Tuesday, it's story time. After that, we don't have anything planned, but Mother Nature might. The mother mountain lion with two kittens has visited us on occasion after dark."

"Would you shoot her," Jerome asked.

Wade turned and asked, "Ben, would you shoot that mountain lion?"

"Of course not. She's just teaching her cubs to survive. All we need to do is clean up real good around here and leave her alone."

YELLOW BEAR

In the spring of 1750, the moon had just come out around the Indian village perched on a slight rise above the Boulder River. An old Indian sat with his small but inquisitive grandson. "Grandfather, are all grizzly bears yellow?"

"No, they're not, Little Feather. Just the ones of the yellow bear clan."

"Tell me the story again, Grandfather, about the big yellow bear."

"Grandson, a long time ago here in our valley where we always camp on our way to the Steaming Mountains, on a night much like this, our village was attacked by a large yellow grizzly bear. He had slipped in quietly and slashed the side of the tipi where the remains of an elk were drying. My grandfather's best dog was the first to reach the bear where he quickly died. When the bear tore the hole in the tipi, he also knocked my grandfather to the ground and with a big slash of his paw, sliced my grandfather's shoulder wide open. The other warriors and the dogs attacked this giant bear, but it picked up the remains of the elk and splashed back over the river with three arrows in it's back.

"The next morning the warriors gathered at grandfather's tipi. They proposed a big hunt to kill the bear. Grandfather agreed but warned them that this bear had very powerful medicine. When examining the prints of the bear, they had discovered that the bear was missing the right rear outside claw. Grandfather's arm was too swollen and the gashes too deep to accompany the warriors on their hunt. They returned three days later with the remains of an elk. They told a story of tracking the bear and seeing it several times until finally he disappeared into the caves on top of the pass that leads into the valley of the Steaming Mountains.

"The braves told stories of the bear's shiny coat, the color of the sun. Some called him Four Claws. Others said that he was Yellow Bear. That was the first of the great yellow bears who lived in this valley. The next time we saw a great yellow bear was many years later when your father and I were hunting for obsidian. Your father was a great, brave warrior. He had killed many enemies and wore the necklace of bear claws proving that he had killed a grizzly all by himself. Sometimes when hunting we would see the paw print of the yellow bear and sometimes we would see it very large and sometimes very small and we began to realize that this missing claw was a sign of the yellow bear clan, passed down from generation to generation. Just like some braves are taller and some are shorter. All these bears born in this valley that have yellow hair, also have a missing claw.

"One day your father and I were hunting obsidian to make new arrowheads on the pass into the valley of the Steaming Mountains. Discovering a cave which gave great promise of obsidian, we very carefully investigated it to be sure there were no bears. First we smelled the air and looked for tracks, both of which would have indicated the presence of a bear. We then built a smoky fire and threw smoky torches into the cave. We waited quietly for hours and then proceeded to take torches into the cave. We could see that it had been used by a bear but not for a long time. We quickly found the place where the obsidian rock lay. Your father began to work the obsidian loose with an antler and I left the cave to get more branches for torches. While I was gone your father gave a loud shout, a cry of surprise. I rushed to the cave just as the giant yellow bear picked him up by the neck. Your father's knife flashed again and again but the great yellow bear wouldn't turn him loose. My arrows didn't seem to hurt him. He just stood there shaking your father until his neck snapped. There was nothing I could do. I fired more arrows but they had no effect.

"Returning to the village I told the story of your brave father's death. The warriors followed me back to the cave and began the hunt. We found the cave had two more entrances. That is how the bear was able to attack your father from behind. You know where your father's burial platform is and you have the bear claw necklace that the warriors gave you after they killed the yellow bear."

"Yes, Grandfather, I do. Please tell me how the warriors killed the great yellow bear."

"Well, my grandson, my arrows must have had some effect. As the braves tracked the bear over the next week, he began to rest more and more until the dogs had him trapped in a small ravine. Longknife, your uncle, with his great spear and his brave heart rushed in to kill the bear that had killed his brother. The spear was driven deep into the bear's chest. The great yellow bear killed two dogs before he began to lose his strength. The warriors just waited. And finally the great yellow bear died. And that's how you got your necklace with the one missing claw. It's powerful medicine so keep it near you always."

"Thank you, Grandfather."

"You're welcome, my grandson. Your father was a brave man and you will be just like him. Now go to Longknife's tipi and curl up in the yellow bear hide with many holes."

CONRAD

It was the middle of July. "Wade, what are you going to do on your one weekend off all summer," Ben asked.

"Nothing exciting. I'm going to Conrad to pick up my kids."

"Yeah, how old are they now?" asked Ben.

"Harvest is thirteen and Canyon is seventeen," Wade replied.

"You had better lock him up or Leigh and Pam will turn him into a real man overnight," Ben said.

"Yeah, I know," he sighed. "Canyon can take care of himself. Besides he'll be bunking with me."

The six hour drive up to Conrad and then out to the ranch gave Wade lots of time to think. Marie was so lovely, such a dramatic contrast to Wendy. He wondered what kind of surprise Wendy and her cronies would cook up when he arrived. Something kinky, no doubt. No more time to worry. There was the driveway to the house.

"Knock, knock, anyone home," he shouted. Canyon and Harvest rushed to the door.

"Hi, Dad," they chorused.

"Give me a hug. I missed you two. Where's your Mom?"

"Downstairs with her friends. I have more packing to do," Harvest said.

"Me too," Canyon said.

"I'll go see your mom. I'll see you in fifteen minutes here at the door," he said. Ducking, so he wouldn't bang his head as he went down the stairs, Wade turned the corner and saw them standing by the bar. Joe, Sharon, Rosie, Jim and Wendy drinking out of tall champagne glasses.

"Wade, welcome. What do you want to drink? Joe asked.

"Nothing, thanks," Wade replied.

"Come on, we're celebrating," Sharon said.

"Good for you," Wade replied.

Turning to Wendy, he said, "Can we talk privately for a few minutes?"

"No, not until you have some champagne," Wendy said as she splashed champagne into a tall crystal glass. "Joe and Sharon just got married."

Wade could not believe his ears. "When did this happen?"

"Yesterday, when their divorces became final," Wendy said. Rosie came over and kissed Wade on the cheek.

Hugging him, she said, "See what I got! A new diamond engagement ring."

Jim stepped up, poked Wade in the ribs and winked. "Are you getting any lately," he asked.

Wade just shook his head. "What about your kids," Wade asked.

"That was easy. The kids and Sharon and I stayed where we were and the guys traded houses," Rosie said. Wife swapping, Wade thought.

"Wendy, can I talk to you upstairs?" Wade asked. On the way up, he turned to her. "Anything I need to know about the kids?"

"No, they're getting along fine, although you might talk to Canyon about studying harder next fall. Just get them back here by noon on the twenty-seventh, two weeks from now. I'll be in

Hawaii for most of the two weeks with George, my new friend." Wade didn't reply.

Canyon and Harvest ran out to the Suburban, tossed their bags in the back and jumped in the front seat. Wade pulled out of the driveway and Harvest asked, "How far is it to the ranch?"

"About six hours, but we're going to stop in Wolf Creek to spend the night with Tim and Jane Forest. You remember them. They visited us about five or six years ago."

"Yeah, right, Dad. Like I was three or four and I'm supposed to remember?"

"Well they live in a place called Cascade in a double wide trailer right on the Missouri River. You can fish almost from their back door."

"Great!" Canyon said. As the miles whistled by, Wade went on to explain that 30 years ago, Tim and Jane bought the Wolf Creek Inn, changed the name to Frenchy's and specialized in French doughnuts served fresh daily. People, among them Wade's family, would drive 50 miles to have a fresh French doughnut with their morning coffee. They had sold Frenchy's just a year ago and had retired to their double wide where Tim watched baseball games and fished and Jane worked in her garden. They arrived just in time to sit down to a typical Montana dinner. Lots of food, well done roast beef, corn, mashed potatoes, homemade bread with honey, pie and ice cream for dessert.

"Wade, let's take a walk out back so I can smoke. Jane won't let me smoke in the house," Tim said.

"Canyon and Harvest, help Jane clean up," Wade said.

"Sure Dad. Then can we go fishing?" Canyon asked.

Tim replied, "Sure, poles are by the back door, ready to go." The two men slipped outside. "Well, Wade, those look like great kids."

"Yes, they are. They seem to be handling the divorce better than I am," Wade said.

Lighting his cigarette, Tim offered Wade a smoke. "No thanks, never have smoked."

Standing there in Tim and Jane's backyard in the warm, late afternoon sunlight, Wade looked over at his friend. "Tim, I can never get used to this river. It's like having a cobra living within ten feet of your house. What is it, two hundred yards wide here and twenty feet deep? It just coils around your place and doesn't make a sound. The Boulder River at the ranch talks to me all the time. Shifting rocks splashing over boulders make a ton of noise. This Missouri River is very scary, like a silent killer."

Tim laughed. "Well you're supposed to respect it. It's the Great MO. We've lived next to her for thirty years and she's become our friend. Anything new in your life Wade?" he asked.

"Just the ranch and maybe my new cook. You might know her. Marie Katerina Bearwalks, out of Depuyer."

"Can't say I do. Bearwalks?"

"That's her maiden name. She was married to an outfitter named Kirk Rudbeck."

"Oh, sure, I know him. That Marie! Now I remember. They had a big fight at the inn one night. He slapped her around pretty good because she was talking to one of my customers. Some of the guys had to hold him down until the highway patrol arrived."

"That's news to me," Wade replied.

"Well, from what I hear, that wasn't the first or the last time. I hear he put her in the hospital with broken ribs and a concussion."

"Well, she's divorced now and he's out of her life."

Just then the kids ran up, their poles ready to go. They had both learned to fish while still babies.

"Dad, Dad, I got one," Harvest yelled after they had been at it for a short time. Canyon frowned and tossed his line further out.

"Harvest, do you want to keep it or toss it back?"

"Keep it, keep it," Harvest shouted as she jumped up and down. "My first fish of the summer," she exclaimed.

With a twinkle in his eye, Tim said, "Jane loves to cook fish for breakfast."

"Gee, thanks," Harvest said. "I would like that." Tim knew Jane hated cooking fish in the morning but Wade figured he was just getting back at her for making him smoke outside.

MEATRACK

"**H**ey, Wade, who you got there," Cindy asked with a smile.

"I would like you to meet my children, Cindy. This is Harvest. She's thirteen, and this is Canyon, he's seventeen. Thought you could put them to work. They're pretty good hands," Wade said.

"Sure can. We're going up to Meatrack with four guests. You guys can help me and Jake saddle up. Wade, why don't you come too? Bill can use the work!"

"Why not," Wade said. Wade had been working all summer with Big Bill. The big, 15 year old ranch horse they acquired in June had never been on mountain trails, and never ridden with a string of horses. He had a lot to learn. He was just getting the hang of spacing himself between horses. The second time Dixie kicked him in the chest he got the idea he shouldn't put his nose on her tail. Bill had the mistaken idea that he should either be in the lead, or go back to the corral. Nothing in between. It was quite comical to watch him and Wade do "helicopters" as Bill spun around and around in the trail, he and Wade having a battle of wills. He had been doing a lot better and a 16 mile ride round trip to the old Indian hunting grounds sure wouldn't hurt him. The Indians had hunted the Meatrack drainage for hundreds of years. This alpine meadow was at 8,500 feet, about six miles long and in places, two miles wide, surrounded by magnificent mountains some as high as 11,000 feet. The dry air and the average daytime temperature of 55 degrees made it the perfect spot to dry strips of elk and deer meat on racks made of poles, thus the name Meatrack. Some of the racks were still standing.

Yellow Bear Lodge had a hunting camp in this beautiful meadow about halfway up the drainage. Summer months they used it for day rides and picnicked, fished or napped among the beautiful wildflowers. In the fall it was their main hunting camp.

"Cindy, we're ready to put the guests up," Jake said. They had done their usual saddling in front of the tack shed with Harvest and Canyon helping. Nine horses stood nose to hitching rail and Jake grabbed a stirrup, kicked his foot in and swung his leg in a graceful motion over the saddle. Jake's job was to sit on his horse about five yards away from the rest of the horses while Cindy helped each rider up into the saddle while discussing the finer points of neck reining and how to keep the ball of your foot in the stirrup. Jake was there for safety reasons to stop anyone in case one of the horses decided to bolt or a guest decided to set out on their own. Cindy helped the last guest up and swung her leg over Apache. Cindy, knowing the pecking order of the horses shouted out, "Julie's behind Jake, then Whiskey, Joe, and Eli. Harvest, you're on Jahaa. Canyon and Dixie are next and Wade, you and Bill are in your favorite spot, last. Just keep him away from Apache or somebody is going to get kicked," Cindy smiled. "Okay Jake, lead them out!"

"Jake," a guest on Julie behind him called out. "How long is this ride up to Meatrack?"

"About three hours up and two hours back," Jake said.

Riding at a leisurely walking pace, crossing streams up and down steep gullies, they reached a point about a mile out where the ranch trail met the main Meatrack trail. Turning right, they crossed the first bridge over Four Mile Creek and headed up the steep embankment which required all the riders to lean forward and hold on to the manes of their horses. This was the first of many climbs before they would reach Meatrack Valley. The wind in the pine trees was the only sound next to the clip clop of the horses hooves, punctuated occasionally by the "rat-a-tat-tat" of the black and white woodpeckers.

Three miles down the trail Jake's sharp eyes spotted a track. "Shit," he whispered. He leaned forward, patted Blackie's neck to get a better look. There it was again, heading up the trail in the same direction they were going. I'll wait another mile, Jake thought, and see what happens.

"Will we see any wild animals," a guest asked Cindy.

"Of course, there are elk, deer and moose up here all the time," Cindy replied.

"Any bears?" the guest asked.

"None this year," she quickly replied. Jake leaned forward again. "Whoa, Blackie," Jake said, as he slipped gracefully to the ground. He reached down and picked up Blackie's front leg, pretending he was looking for a rock caught in a shoe. In reality, he was inspecting a very nice grizzly bear paw print in the mud.

"Everything okay?" Cindy asked.

"Yessum I think it's cinch checking time," Jake replied as he proceeded down the line of horses checking each guest's cinch. He continued until he got to Cindy's where he proceeded to check her. She looked at him like he was crazy. Her cinch was fine and she knew it. Jake leaned in close to her leg. "There is a yellow grizzly bear on the trail up ahead of us about a half hour, by my guess, and maybe she has a cub. The real dangerous type. I'll tell Wade." Moving to the end of the line, Jake checked Wade's cinch.

Wade leaned forward and whispered, "I've seen one track, but there are too many horses ahead of me to recognize it. What have we got, another mountain lion?" Wade asked.

"No, worse. A yellow grizzly bear, the one with the missing right rear claw and maybe a cub."

"How close?"

"Few minutes, to a half hour ahead of us. Shall we go back?" Wade thought, we haven't had trouble with bears in years but it hadn't rained in a long time and there wasn't much of a berry crop.

"Is your rifle loaded," Wade asked.

"Yes, sir."

"Okay, let's go. Take it real easy, no surprises," Wade said. Jake turned and started up the trail toward Blackie. Blackie's ears were back, his nose in the air. He must have caught a whiff of the bear. Somewhere in Blackie's background, he had had a disastrous experience with a bear. Jake had seen the scar marks on his left flank and had wondered if it was a bear or a lion. Jake talked softly to Blackie to calm him down and swung his leg up over the saddle. He started up the trail very slowly, keeping his eyes open for any movement or any further tracks. When they reached the lower end of Meatrack meadow, the tracks disappeared off to the left of the trail. Jake turned and caught Cindy's eye and nodded his head to the left. Cindy quickly spotted the tracks and turned and gave Wade a nod. They moved slowly and quietly up the trail into Meatrack meadow. Tying the horses to a small grove of pine trees, everyone got down to stretch their legs again. Most walked in that rolling cowboy gait with bowed legs. Breaking out fishing gear and lunches, Harvest and Canyon lent a hand and helped distribute the individually packed lunches.

"Harvest, Canyon, bring your lunches and come with me. I'll show you where you can find some petrified wood," Wade said. The guests spread out fishing, eating lunch or taking pictures of wildflowers.

"Jake, let's go for a walk," Cindy offered. Jake's quick glance told him that the horses were okay. He grabbed his lunch and followed Cindy down to the stream. The sunlight and the altitude gave the meadow wildflowers a golden hue. Sprinkled across the valley were boulders and high alpine flowers in blue, yellow, red, and white growing in clusters.

"Look, look, Jake. Here's a group of Elephant Heads. Do you know how rare they are?" Looking down at the flower Jake could see what appeared to be a series of purple Elephant Heads, one below the other attached to the main stem. "These only grow above eight thousand feet and only bloom for a short time. It's good luck to find them."

Just then, Jake and Cindy heard the high pitched whinny of a horse in distress. Jake broke into a run, arms pumping, legs stretched out, as he leaped over logs and boulders in the stream. Cindy was hot on his heels. As Jake rounded the corner of the small grove of pine trees, he saw in a glance what the trouble was. Blackie had panicked and stepped over his lead rope because a grizzly bear had just stood up a 100 yards upstream. In one swift movement, Jake jerked the lead rope that was tied around the tree, popped the bowline knot and grabbed his rifle out of the scabbard. Blackie reared, breaking the halter. Jake grabbed for the reins but missed. Blackie was gone in a flash down the trail, back to the corral at the ranch. Jake had never taken his eye off the grizzly. He levered a shell into the chamber and said quietly, "You all mount up. It looks like this valley belongs to a grizzly bear today." Guests were quickly clicking off pictures of the first and probably only grizzly bear they would see in their lifetimes.

"That's enough everybody," Cindy commanded. "We've got to go. Mount up now. You too, Jake. Get up behind me."

"No, I'll walk. You take the guests down!"

"No, I won't. I'm not leaving you here alone on this trail, on foot, with a grizzly bear. Get up behind me," she commanded as she kicked her foot out of the stirrup.

"I'll lead," Wade said. "Let's go." Wade and Big Bill took off and the guests fell in behind with some difficulty as their horses, who were sidestepping nervously with big eyes, were trying to watch every movement the bear made.

Just then Jake realized he had a bigger problem than just a Grizzly bear. He had a rifle in one hand and couldn't figure out where to put his other hand. When Cindy leaned back into him and said, "Hang on," she kicked Apache who jumped with a little buck to protest the extra weight. Jake firmly grasped Cindy's waist. He looked back over his shoulder, then leaned forward and whispered in Cindy's ear, "It's not the same bear. The tracks I saw earlier were different. This guy behind us is about twelve hundred pounds. The other one was about half his size."

"Great. Now you're telling me we have one large grizzly behind us and one mean mother bear with cub in front of us? This started out as such a wonderful day!" With that, Cindy leaned back into Jake's chest. Jake's one arm held on tight to her waist while his other with the rifle in it swung up and down beside Apache's flank. They moved quickly down the trail and Apache fell into a walk, slowly turning into a rocking motion carrying his double load. Jake could feel the sensation in his crotch as the rolling motion rode him up against Cindy's firm bottom. His manhood began to spring to life. Shit, out of the frying pan and into the fire. It's going to be a long two hours down this trail to the corral!

I think he likes me, thought Cindy, as she pushed further back in the saddle into his erection. After 45 minutes, Jake couldn't take it any more. He slid off the back of Apache and quickly turned around looking back up the trail and allowing the bulge in his pants to subside. "I'll walk from here."

"No, you can't keep up with the horses," Cindy replied.

"Just let me try for a while. Here, you take the rifle." So they proceeded down the trail with Jake walking a mile, then riding a mile, or for as long as he could take it. Cindy was having the time of her life!

Over dinner, the grizzly bear story was told over and over and grew until even Jake and Cindy didn't recognize it. Jake relaxed and put his feet up on the coffee table knowing that Blackie was in the corral with the other horses and nothing had happened to the guests, Wade's kids or Cindy. Cindy sat quietly thinking, maybe this Jake's not such a bad guy after all. Shy, but he sure doesn't panic when there is danger about. He's got a cool head and knows the wilderness. Besides, he seems to have a larger than normal bulge in his jeans!

HIGH MEADOW

"Am I on time," Wade asked, as he poked his head through the kitchen door.

"Of course you are," Marie replied. "The cookies always come out at eleven thirty every morning. And who always walks in precisely at eleven thirty? My quality control inspector, who else?"

"What's for today?"

"Peanut butter and chocolate chip," she said. "Which do you prefer?"

"Hmm, ouch, they're hot! Too much peanut butter in this one and not enough chocolate chips in this one," Wade said, laughing.

"Get out of my kitchen." Marie replied, gesturing with a broom and a smile. Wade ducked and stepped out onto the porch.

"What are you doing Saturday afternoon? The guests are going to be gone all day on a four-by-four trip or an all day ride to Meatrack."

"Resting, taking a nap. What do you have in mind?"

"You haven't had a chance to ride up to the high meadow yet this year. We can leave after breakfast as soon as you get the picnic lunches made. I'll get you back in time to start dinner around four."

"Sounds like fun. I'll make us a lunch," she said.

Saturday came. The trail to the high meadow rambled along the edge of the river. Wade and Marie watched a Cutthroat trout flash through the water snatching a mayfly out of the air.

"Marie, how is Julie doing today," Wade asked.

"Just great, she's my favorite horse," Marie replied.

"Once we get to the top of these switchbacks, we'll stop and I'll show you a fantastic view of the ranch and the river."

After a half hour of steady climbing, Wade and Marie tied the horses to some lodge pole pines and walked hand in hand to the edge of a cliff. They looked down on the river sparkling in the sunlight 400 feet below. They could see up and down the valley for miles.

"Look," shouted Marie, "an eagle." It slowly rode the wind currents looking for trout. Wade encircled Marie in his arms.

"Are you happy?" he whispered against her neck.

"Yes, very," she replied.

"Me too," he whispered as he gently kissed the side of her neck sending shivers and goose bumps up and down her body. She felt a warm sensation all over and fought back the urge to tear his clothes off. The moment was just too perfect.

Holding her a little tighter Wade whispered, "In another half an hour we'll be at the top and can have lunch. I'll start with dessert first, just like the French do."

"I know what you have in mind, Wade. We'll see."

As they reached the end of the last set of switchbacks Wade stopped to let the horses blow. "We'll ride to the top of the meadow where you can see the ranch, the river and the entire valley. I've been watching the trail and no one's been up here in several days."

Later, their bodies glistened in the sun as they lay entwined on top of the horse blankets. "Oh Wade, just hold me," Marie said as she snuggled closer. Wade began to kiss her ear and the side of her neck, slowly tracing a finger along her breast and gently flicking her nipple.

"You're feeling frisky again. I thought we just made love," Marie said.

"I can never get enough of you." Wade gently rolled Marie onto her back and began kissing his way down her throat to the valley between her breasts, taking time to caress each nipple, passing her navel down to her soft furry mound. The smells and the tastes of making love in the outdoors high in the mountains made Wade forget everything except Marie's little mews that began to grow louder and louder as his tongue quickly flicked over and found her center. Placing his hands on each side of her bottom, he completely buried his face. Her mews now were moans of pleasure.

"Oh, ohh, ohhh!" Tossing her head from side to side, she arched her back until she fell exhausted on the horse blankets. Wade rose, kissed her face and entered her slowly letting the sensations fill her first and then himself. He came with a loud shout and a groan that made any nearby coyotes envious.

Marie woke hours later looking at the white puffy clouds drifting by. She kissed Wade awake. "We have to start back," she said. "Dinner can't be late."

The eagle made a leisurely circle in the sky over the high meadow. With a gentle flap of his wings, he headed south toward Meatrack meadow 10 miles away. As he came upon the meadow he could see Jake and Cindy and four guests dismounting and tying their horses in a stand of trees.

"Jake, here we are again at my favorite place on earth, Meatrack Meadow," Cindy said with her arms outstretched walking in a tiny circle.

The trip up was uneventful. Jake and Cindy as guides took turns passing out lunches and rigging fishing poles for the guests.

"After everyone gets settled Jake, let's go for a walk," Cindy said.

Jake didn't answer but walked over to Blackie, checked his lead rope and quickly drew his gun from the scabbard. "Okay, let's go," Jake said.

"Jake, that grizzly bear is long gone."

"Don't want to take no chances," he said.

"Okay, follow me." Cindy tried to take his hand, but Jake pulled away. Around the bend in the stream, they walked side by side into a small meadow of wildflowers swaying gently in the breeze. "Sit here beside me, Jake," she said as she patted a log. Jake sat down in front of the log, leaned back and used it as a pillow.

He pulled his hat over his eyes. "Nap time," he said.

"No you don't. I want to talk."

"Go ahead," Jake replied.

"No, I want you to talk. Tell me everything about you," she said.

"Nothing to tell," Jake grumbled.

Putting her hands on her hips, she glared down at the top of his hat. "There sure is. Did you have a girlfriend in high school?"

"Nope."

"Did you have a date?"

"Nope."

"Jake, that's just not true, so tell me the truth, or I'll never let you get to sleep."

Jake thought several minutes before he started to tell his story about Angelica. He talked for almost an hour. The words flowed out of him like a river that had just busted through a dam. As he finished, he began to cry. His heart was still broken.

Cindy wrapped her arms around him, holding him and rocking him. "Not all women are like that. Some of us take very good care of our men. Next time we come up here, I'll tell you why I never married. Let's just watch the clouds go by. Look. A butterfly has just landed on your knee. It's good luck."

Jake thought, it's time to be free of Angelica. She's gone forever. And Cindy smelled very good and felt good too. Yeah, she was one nice lady.

KIRK

One phone call and one day changed Marie's whole world. Kirk, her ex-husband called informing her he was coming out to the ranch and needed to see her on a very important matter. She immediately began to worry about his intentions. But it was breakfast time at the ranch and she couldn't miss the eight o'clock deadline to serve, so back to work she went on the "sticky" buns she had set up the night before.

Wade spoke to the Taylor family. "You know the rules. Guests always eat first, than the staff, me and then the cook. Please start and keep in mind that my staff all carry knives and they're really hungry," he said with a smile. That usually got some chuckles out of the newcomers. The buffet breakfast went smoothly as usual, though Marie took no notice of the raves over her sticky buns. She was too preoccupied by Kirk's menacing call.

"Don't forget horseback riding starts at nine at the corral. Hikers to the Indian Caves, meet at the lodge at nine thirty. Flyfishing lessons will start at the pond at four and dinner is at six, here at the lodge," Cindy announced in a loud voice as she organized the activities.

"The float trip is tomorrow, weather permitting. Expert horseback riders will leave at nine thirty tomorrow for their all day ride. Dress warmly and in layers with hats, mosquito repellant and suntan lotion. See you all later! Don't forget the sign up list on the door," Cindy shouted as she walked out of the lodge.

Marie whispered to Wade, "Can I see you outside?"

"Sure."

Each grabbed a plastic bag of garbage and walked slowly to the garbage hut. "Wade, my ex-husband is coming tonight and he's very jealous."

"Aren't you divorced?"

"Yes, but he said he wants to see me about something important and he wouldn't say what. I'm sure he's still jealous. What you and I have Wade is really wonderful, but let's just act like friends while he's around until I find out what he wants. I guess I'm still frightened from the time in Browning when he almost killed a guy who just wanted to dance with me."

Tossing the garbage into the bear proof building, Wade said, "Fine, just let me know what's going on."

Squeezing Wade's hand, Marie said, "Thanks" on her way back to the kitchen.

The rest of the day went smoothly. The eight New Yorkers were getting along fine with the two couples from Oklahoma. Although Wade had a difficult time understanding the accents, especially when the New Yorkers started talking with an Oklahoma accent. Laughing to himself, Wade thought about the other night at the bar after the rodeo when the red headed matriarch of the New York clan had overheard a local mountain man say, "Hey, ain't that a New York accent?" She had turned to the Montana mountain man and said, "You want a New York Accent? I'll give you a New York accent!" And using a time honored obscene gesture she said, "Up yours!" The whole bar had laughed and ever since that night, she had been teaching Wade's staff how to say "Up yours!" with a New York accent. Laughter was wonderful on the ranch.

Kirk arrived about eight o'clock, walking out of the woods quietly into the light of the campfire. Marie was startled and jumped up, introducing him as her former husband to Wade, the staff and guests. Kirk, being his charming self, joined in the songs, and after the music quieted down told the story about the Yellow Bear Valley and how it got it's name.

"The way I've got it figured, is the reason the Indians, the sheep herders and the miners couldn't ever find those yellow grizzly bears was because they had a hideout that nobody knew about. Wade, you know that Nelson mine just above Independence, the one high up on the hill, north side of the road, just down from Baboon Peak?"

"Yes," Wade replied.

"I was up there last week looking for some sheep. I found another way into the mine. Actually, it was an old cave, and just another hundred yards across the ridge there was another entrance. Both of those old caves lead down into a mine shaft. Inside the first cave was a very old bear den. Bears and shit as old as the mountains. Even an old Griz skull. Next time you take a group up to Blue Lake, look for yourself."

The campfire slowly broke up with couples and families going back to their cabins. "Marie, come for a ride with me so we can talk." Kirk grabbed her tightly by the arm and walked her toward his pickup parked down in the trees. Wade watched quietly and thought, she can handle him. She did for four years. Marie reluctantly got in. Kirk drove down the driveway and turned toward the wilderness away from the ranch and town.

"Kirk, what did you want to talk about?"

"I'm leaving the state, going to Arizona. I've got a new job."

"Doing what?"

"Outfitting and guiding," Kirk explained as he turned into a deserted campground. Stopping the truck, he turned off the engine and the lights. Kirk turned to Marie and said, "I really missed you!"

"Okay, you might be telling the truth, Kirk, but you hurt me, and it's over forever between us."

"I love you and I've changed. I've had counseling. You'll see."

"Maybe you have. When you get to Arizona, send me your address and maybe I'll write you a letter. If that's all you had to tell me, let's go back to the ranch."

Starting the engine, Kirk turned to Marie. "Just a kiss goodbye?" It all happened so fast, Marie wasn't prepared when he grabbed her by the neck and placed his hard calloused hand up the front of her shirt, ripping it open, exposing her breasts. Kissing her hard he forced her flat onto the seat of the pickup. Marie fought back but she was no match for this 6'4", 230 pound mountain man. Before she knew it, he had her pants down, his knee between her legs and had entered her. Grasping for anything to make him get off, she found a flashlight on the floor of the truck. With all of her strength she hit him hard several times on the top of his head. As he raised his head, she hit him again harder and broke his nose. He yelled and rolled off her. She scrambled out of the cab, grabbing what clothes she could, and ran for the ranch. She had just started up the driveway when Kirk's pickup lights caught her. She jumped behind a large rock. He braked to a sliding stop and shouted, "You bitch! I'll get even. I have a big surprise for you. I've got the clap! Now you do too!" Sneering, he said, "At least I think it's the clap. It could be worse. See you later, bitch." Throwing dirt into the air, he tore down the road. Marie fell to her knees crying.

Then, putting on her torn clothes, she staggered to her feet and began the long walk to the bunkhouse. What can I do, she thought. Kirk couldn't be that mean. Yes, he could. Marie leaned against a tree gathering her thoughts and emotions. Her sobs subsided. Catching her breath, she looked around and then rushed into the bunkhouse, shutting the door quickly behind her. I need a shower, she sighed. Dropping her clothes to the floor, she slipped into a robe. With the hot water pounding on her back, she washed herself three times. Think. What can I do? See a doctor? Tell Wade? No! See a doctor in Big Timber, maybe. No, everyone in town would find out. Then, it's Billings on my next day off, Saturday. But doctors aren't open on Saturday. I'll have to go Monday. I know, I'll trade with Anna. I feel like I'm going to die. Back in her room Marie cried herself to sleep.

Five o'clock came way too early for Marie. After showering again she carefully applied her makeup to cover the bruise on her cheek. She walked quietly out of the bunkhouse taking strong, determined steps toward the lodge to begin cooking. Breakfast was a nightmare and Marie did everything she could to avoid Wade. Sitting with the guests, she kept up a constant chatter only looking up once at Wade. Wade's smile almost broke her heart and she returned it with a frown.

Later after lunch, Wade stepped into the kitchen. He decided not to ask how her meeting with Kirk went. If she wanted to talk about it, he would listen, but better leave sleeping dogs lie. On to bigger and better things. "Are you going to the Road Kill Saturday night?"

"No!"

"But Saturday is your day off."

"No! It's Monday. I've changed days with Anna." Marie thought, I can't tell him.

"You could come down later, after dinner. I'll even wait for you."

"No, you won't. Just go yourself and have a good time. I've got things to do. Get out of my kitchen so I can clean the floor."

"Did everything go okay with Kirk," he blurted out. This was so unlike her, he thought. What was wrong?

"Fine, just fine. Just leave me alone." She turned her back on him, afraid she couldn't keep the tears from filling her eyes and started cleaning the stove.

Wade walked away, shaking his head. I'll never understand women. Bobo brushed his leg just as one of the guests approached him. "Are you teaching flyfishing this afternoon?"

"You bet," replied Wade. "Just sign up on the board behind the door and I'll see you at four."

Later on in the week while still trying to figure out Marie's sudden coolness, Wade picked up the phone. "Hello, is that you, Shirley? Wade here. I'm calling to tell you the septic line is finished and you can come inspect it any time. Thanks for making that a warning instead of a ticket."

"You're welcome. What are your plans for Saturday?"

"Well, I'm going to the dance. How about I pick you up around six and we'll stop here on our way down and you can inspect the line."

"That's great! See you then." Hanging up the phone, Shirley thought, Wow! I finally get him alone for two hours, an hour down and an hour back. I should be able to start his heart in that amount of time. Shirley fantasized the rest of the afternoon about where they would park, the color of the moon, what she would wear, her new red bra and matching panties, how soft his lips would be, how strong his muscles. She finally sought relief in a hot bath with her very finely skilled fingers.

MARIE'S SATURDAY NIGHT

Shaved, showered and wearing his new shirt, Wade petted Bobo and explained he had to stay behind and protect the ranch. Bobo looked like he understood, turning his head a little to the left so his ear fell over his eye.

The trip to the Four Mile Ranger Station was a short two miles. Just before the gate where a little spring crossed the road, making it necessary to come to a complete stop, Wade saw something that made his heart jump. A set of grizzly bear tracks and big ones, with the right rear outside claw missing. There hadn't been any sign of this killer bear in years. The last time was two years ago when he broke into an RV at Independence. Now the bear is down here, thought Wade. Only 15 miles from Independence, the tracks looked fresh and headed down river, probably to that huckleberry patch just across from the ranch. Wade took a deep breath and tried not to think about it.

Shirley was ready and she was a knockout with a low cut peasant blouse and tight jeans that left little to the imagination. She jumped into the Suburban and gave Wade a kiss on the cheek.

"Thanks for picking me up. Let's go."

Wade discussed the yellow bear tracks on the way back to the ranch. He was concerned about leaving Marie alone while everyone was at the dance. While Shirley inspected the septic line, Wade found Marie reading in the bunkhouse.

"Marie, would you please change your mind?" Wade asked after he explained about the yellow bear tracks.

"No I won't. I've lived in the mountains with grizzly bears all my life. I'm fully capable of taking care of myself. You're leaving Bobo here and with the outfitter's dogs next door, I'll be fine."

Wade left with a heavy heart. Marie, watching out the window, saw Shirley lean over and give Wade another kiss on the cheek. Tears formed in the corner of her eyes.

I can't tell him. I'm too ashamed. I don't own him, she thought. "Here Bobo, come and sleep in my room tonight."

The Suburban hit a rut and Shirley placed her hand on Wade's knee. He looked down and frowned. Shirley said, "I need something to hold onto. Is this all right?" Wade just grunted.

The Road Kill was alive this Saturday night. Tourists, locals, Leprechaun Jim, Bubba Bill, and Noble Tweedy were all sitting on the porch rail. Wade walked up to Noble and said, "Are you going to tell the story of yellow bear tonight? I just saw his tracks two miles above the ranch." Noble couldn't resist that introduction and immediately began his story.

With her back against the wall, Marie was sitting on her bed reading a new book. How did this happen to me, she thought. Every one's off to the Road Kill having a great time. I almost threw Wade into that slut Shirley's arms. I hope he's strong. This feeling in my stomach tells me if she gets him alone, and gets her hooks in him, I'll never get him back. Me, sitting here with this stuff growing inside me, having to wait until Monday."

Marie was so absorbed in her thoughts, she didn't notice Bobo's hair stand up on his back as his nose sniffed the air. After his second growl, he got Marie's attention. "What is it, Bobo,"

Marie asked, as she listened. Probably just the wind. Bobo quieted down and Marie went back to her book.

But the yellow grizzly bear with the missing claw was on the ranch. He had just pried open the door to the garbage shed. Sinking his teeth into a black plastic garbage sack, he tore it open. A single garbage sack wasn't much of a meal for a 1,200 pound grizzly bear. The garbage shed was mostly empty because Wade had just finished a garbage run down to Camp-on-the-Boulder and had dumped the whole week's worth into their bear proof container.

The grizzly made quick work of the garbage sack and began to look for more. His nose was working overtime. Experts say that the difference between what people can smell and what a grizzly bear can smell is the difference between a postage stamp and a football field. His nose quickly picked up the fresh garbage smell from the Friday night cook-out stored by mistake in the bunkhouse. Wade hadn't picked it up because he didn't know it was there. Left over steak and huckleberry pie was like putting out an odor sign in capital letters saying, "Bear dinner served." Huckleberries were a food staple for bears in the fall of the year.

Marie and Bobo had fallen asleep on the bed when the yellow grizzly bear's 1,200 pounds hit the front door of the bunkhouse like a runaway train. Both of the giant paws slammed the door off it's hinges. Bobo leaped from the bed and rushed to the door, barking. Marie, slower to wake, took a few seconds to figure out what happened. "Okay, you guys, hold it down, I'm trying to sleep in here," she shouted.

The grizzly began tearing the garbage apart with swift rips of his paws. Bobo was going crazy crashing into the bedroom door. Marie quietly opened the door and a flash of black and white spots leapt through the opening, landing squarely on the back of the Grizzly, sinking his teeth into the bear's neck. This was a fight to the death and Bobo didn't stand much of a chance. Marie could only see the hind legs and stomach of the bear through the door. It was so huge, it's body completely filled the doorway.

Meanwhile, Shirley had Wade by the hand and had pulled him onto the dance floor. Shirley sighed to herself as she pushed her crotch against his leg and felt him begin to stir. Several dances later Wade suggested they get a beer and go outside to cool off on the porch. Noble had just finished the yellow bear story. "Wade, will you walk me over to the Suburban, please? I need something out of my purse."

The cool night air felt good on his shoulders as he unlocked the door for Shirley. Reaching in and picking up her purse, she turned halfway and kissed Wade full on the lips. At first he was surprised but soon began to relax as her tongue explored his mouth. Her body pressed tightly against his as she pressed him against the Suburban door. He began to get aroused. Shirley reached up and put his hand on her breast. He could feel the nipple grow under his touch. She began to rub his crotch. He was beginning to lose it.

Wade gently pushed her back and said, "Not here, not now. Let's go back to the dance." He walked away leaving Shirley trying to straighten her blouse and re-do her lipstick. Wade thought, I can't be alone with this woman all the way back to the ranch tonight. There's no telling what she might do. And no matter what I do, I'm going to get in trouble. I don't need another woman, let alone a Forest Service agent mad at me. As Wade stepped up to the porch and into the door, Ben Johnson grabbed him by the arm.

"We have got a potential problem about to happen. Those two college girls we hired aren't used to drinking at this altitude and we got a couple of mountain men that haven't seen women in several months. I think they look an awful lot like honey to a bear. Why don't you give them a ride back and I'll drive their car up."

Wade said, "Great, let's go get them."

The bear swung Bobo around, glancing him off the wall. On the second time around, Bobo hit the staircase and lost his grip on the bear's neck. Landing on his feet, facing the bear with his back to the bedroom door, Bobo bared his teeth and growled. The bear stood up, blocking the outside door. Bobo barked and growled and made a lunge for the bear's throat, but missed. Bobo was quick and ducked under the paw that flashed over his head.

No gun, God dammit. They're all upstairs in Cindy's room. I have to get out, Marie thought. Just then she heard a yelp and saw Bobo smashed into the wall as the bear stuck his head into her room. The difference between a black bear and a grizzly is most of the time you can frighten a black bear by standing up to it. But not a Grizzly. Once he gets mad, he goes berserk and doesn't quit. Escape, thought Marie. The bear turned his head to check the garbage and Bobo. At that moment, Marie flung a chair into the window, smashing it, and dove headfirst as the bear bit her boot.

Hanging upside down, Marie reached up to untie her boot. With all her strength she pushed against the wall with her free leg and pulled her other leg with her hands. Her foot was being crushed. The blood from her cut leg seemed to excite the bear even more. But as it opened its mouth for another bite, Marie fell free into a bed of pine needles. The bear crashed against the window frame, shaking the entire bunkhouse. Marie had only a few seconds to find safety as the bear growled and slammed against the window sill again. It began to crack.

Moving quickly, Marie rolled under the bunkhouse that sat 18" above the ground. Crawling to the far corner and bleeding badly, she fainted. Meanwhile the grizzly banged against the window sill and it split, giving the bear just enough room to slide out. His nose took him to the trail of blood Marie had left behind, and he began to dig.

Back in the bunkhouse, Bobo slowly got up. Running to the window on shaky legs, he began to bark as he saw the bear digging under the house. Then Bobo jumped back, dashed out the front door and around the corner. Coming up behind the bear, he sank his teeth into the soft inner part of the bear's thigh. The bear whirled and charged. Bobo won the race for the first 10 yards but his speed was diminishing. Now Bobo and the bear were standing about five yards apart, baring their teeth and growling. The bear then stood up, growled and charged, but Bobo outran him. This process was repeated over and over, but each time the bear was getting closer. They were about a mile from the bunkhouse on the main road when the bear charged again and didn't stop. The big paw crushed Bobo's skull instantly.

Back at the Road Kill, Wade and Ben were loading two very drunk young ladies into the Suburban. Pam tried to jump out and go back in screaming that she was more than enough for all those mountain men. Wade got her back down in the back seat, snapped the seatbelt on her and started back up the road. She was so drunk she couldn't figure out how to release it.

Miles later, the headlights of the Suburban washed over a large animal. Grizzly bear and feeding, flashed in Wade's mind. This was very dangerous. Screeching to a halt Wade shouted, "Grizzly Bear! Don't anyone get out." His sleepy passengers came instantly awake.

The bear continued to feed, but it was only a few minutes before it walked across the road and down the hill to the river. Must have been a road kill deer. Those bears are scavengers and opportunists, Wade thought, as he put the car into gear and drove up the road. Looking out his window his heart stopped. The girls began to scream, "Bobo, Bobo!"

"Don't get out. We have to get to the ranch," Wade shouted. "Bobo's too much of a mountain dog to get caught unless something else was going on." Gravel flying, the Suburban slid around corners and pulled to a halt in front of the tipi. Wade sprinted up the hill to get his 30.06 and his 357 Magnum and Ben opened the door to his pickup and pulled out his rifle.

"Ben, you escort the girls to the bunkhouse. Cindy, Jake and I will inspect the lodge."

Flashlights in hand, they reached the lodge. Jake hollered, "Over here at the garbage shed." They stopped and rushed toward the bunkhouse when they heard Leigh and Pam scream. In a glance they took in the damage. The busted front door, the door to Marie's bedroom open, the window broken and the window frame smashed. Fresh blood glistened on the window sill.

With Ben and Jake's tracking skill, it didn't take them long to figure out what happened.

"Marie must be around here somewhere," Wade said, as they all began to call her name. No response. Ben went around to check underneath the window and dropped to his knees to inspect the hole he found. His light flashed on Marie curled up in the far corner.

"I've got her," he shouted and within a few minutes they had pulled her out. She regained consciousness as they were washing her foot and leg.

"Bobo saved my life," she whispered. "My leg?"

"It's not too bad," Wade said, holding her in his arms. We'll get you to town as quickly as possible."

DEATH AND YELLOW BEAR

Marie was quickly taken to Billings in an ambulance. Bear bites were much too infectious to be treated at the clinic in Big Timber. Wade, Shirley, Bill Grant from Fish and Game, and Deputy Sheriff Sam Tibbin, were all gathered in the lobby of the Grand Hotel in Big Timber to decide what to do. "We'll need some different dogs. My usual tracker is working on a cat hunt over by Dillon. Anyone got any suggestions," Bill asked.

Just then, Kirk slammed his way through the front door. "What the hell happened to Marie? Wade, can't you protect your women up there on that pussy ranch?" Wade bristled. Shirley quickly put her hand on his arm and held him back.

"We're organizing a bear hunt," Bill explained.

"I'm the best bear hunter in the state," Kirk shouted. "I've hunted bears in the Bob Marshall and Glacier Park and big ones too."

"That's great, Kirk, but we need someone like Wade who knows the Absorkees," Bill said.

"What do you mean! I just finished logging that upper Boulder. I've been all over those mountains every day. That pissant stays on that pussy ranch all day. I'll find you that bear," Kirk said.

With that, Wade couldn't take it anymore and he exploded. He grabbed Kirk by the shirt and slammed him hard against the wall. Kirk threw a punch and Wade ducked and slammed him against the wall again. Shirley, Bill and Sam jumped into the fracas and pulled the two apart.

"All right, cut it out," Bill said. "Let's all meet at the ranch at daylight and start from there. You all know the rules about hunting grizzly bears. They are protected under the Endangered Species Act, until they attack a human. Now I can authorize a full hunt. Maybe we can round up some dogs. Shirley, you contact the Search and Rescue and put them on alert."

"I ain't waiting around for no daylight. That bear bit my ex-wife and I'm going to kill him," Kirk shouted as he banged out the door.

"I'll go talk to Kirk and keep him from going off half cocked," Sam said. "See you at six." Sam headed out the door. "Kirk, wait up. Where are you going to begin the hunt?"

"None of your fucking business," Kirk shouted.

"Kirk, we need to know. It's a big wilderness and if something happens, we need to know where you are," Sam replied.

"I hunt alone and where I want," Kirk said as he got into his pickup.

As daylight filtered in between the big peaks at the ranch, Wade was explaining, "My staff saw two grizzly bears up Meatrack last week. Neither were aggressive, but you never know." The group of hunters had formed a semi-circle around the bunkhouse where the bear had broken the window and dug down under the foundation.

Ben leaned over and examined the track. "It's going to be easy to track this guy. He's missing a claw."

"Well, Ben," Wade said, "It might not be that easy. We see lots of that type of track around here and the legend says all these yellow grizzly bears have that claw missing, so I'd be very careful tracking one bear when another one behind you might be the killer. We'll begin tracking down where Bobo died."

"I'm sorry for your loss, Wade," Bill Grant said.

"Thanks, Bill. It's okay though, because Bobo did his job the best he could. I buried him early this morning."

"I got a line on some dogs over on the Stillwater. Butch Mathias will bring them over tomorrow or the next day. They chase bears and lions," Bill said.

Kirk had left Big Timber hours earlier and headed up to his logging camp to get supplies and his larger rifle. On his way up he stopped at the spot where the bear had killed Bobo. With his flashlight he picked up the trail and tracked the bear down to the river, noting how easy it would be with this bear with the missing claw. Once the bear crossed the river, he could be anywhere. What's that moving over there, Kirk thought. His flashlight caught a glimpse of fur. He fired, heard a growl and then nothing. I think I hit him. Great, a wounded grizzly bear! I'm not crossing this river tonight. I'll just leave this little trap for Wade and the boys. They'll enjoy going into the brush after a wounded grizzly.

Back in his pickup Kirk began to think, now that I've put a hole in him, this bear will go into the high country. Probably to the caves to lick his wounds. I'll head for the Upside Down Trail which is about half way between where I shot the bear and the caves, he thought. If I can cross his trail, I can follow him.

Later, Ben and Wade looked at each other as they spotted the tracks of a man's boot next to the pool of blood where Bobo had died.

"Someone was here last night. He followed the bear tracks and then came back," Ben said. "What do you think, Wade?"

"It's probably Kirk," Sam replied. "He's got more guts than sense, tracking a mean bear at night. He never did tell me where he was going to hunt, the stupid son-of-a-bitch!"

They then followed the tracks down the meadow and up to the river's edge. It took them another hour before Jake found the tracks on the other side leading up Hawley Creek Tail. "You guys better come over here and see this," Jake hollered, as he began to move in a slow circle. Jake levered a shell into his rifle.

"What's up, Jake," Wade asked.

"The Fish and Game guy better take a look under that fir tree, Jake said. What Bill saw made his blood run cold. Fur, blood, bear urine, claw marks and prints just like the bear prints by Bobo. Turning to Wade, Bill asked, "Did Marie say she shot the bear?"

"No, she didn't have a gun," Wade replied.

"Someone shot him and didn't do a very good job," Bill said.

"Shit," Ben said. "Now we've got ourselves a wounded grizzly bear. The most dangerous combination in North America."

"Okay guys, let's back out of here slow and easy," Bill said. "We'll come back with the dogs."

"Who the hell would shoot a grizzly bear in the dark and not tell anybody," Wade asked.

"Two guesses. First one doesn't count," Ben replied.

"Let's go back to the lodge and do some planning," Bill said.

"Ben, you and I can get some horses and ride up the other side of Hawley Creek Trail and warn any backpackers," Jake said. Ben looked at Jake like he was crazy but realized he was right.

"Okay, but I want some of the Fish and Game 00 buck shot shells for my shotgun."

Bill patted Ben on the shoulder. "You'll get all the shells you need."

About that time, Marie, floating in a Demerol haze, heard a light knock on the door of her room at the hospital. Her doctor walked in and asked, "How do you feel?"

"Not too good," she replied.

"Well, we've given you a complete exam and you've got a bad cut on your leg but it will heal leaving only a tiny scar. Your big toe is broken and you have puncture wounds on the bottom and side of your foot. These are serious because of the chance of infection, but we'll watch them closely and we're quite sure you'll be okay.

"Miss Bearwalks, last night you were pretty out of it, but you kept saying over and over, more tests, more tests, I'm very sick. Is there something else I should know," the doctor asked. Marie nodded and began to cry. The doctor leaned over and she whispered in his ear. "We'll run the tests today and we should know by tomorrow. You just rest and you'll be fine.

Λ Λ Λ

Kirk arrived back at his logging camp in the early afternoon. He packed three days worth of supplies and set off at a fast pace towards the caves. A day later Kirk picked up the bear's trail heading for the caves on Baboon Mountain. Kirk had discovered the caves while exploring Baboon Peak looking for trees to log. He had found that the cave had several entrances because two of the mine shafts were connected from the other side of the mountain.

It was late afternoon when Kirk arrived at one of the entrances. He built a smoky fire just like the Indians had, and began throwing burning branches into the cave. But unlike the Indians, who sat back for hours and waited to see if a bear would come out, Kirk had little patience and waited less than 15 minutes before he stepped into the mouth of the cave. Flashlight in one hand, rifle in the other, he walked quietly and quickly into the depths. His flashlight reflected off bones, bear scat, bear beds dug out of dirt and small tufts of fur clinging to the edges of some of the rocks.

He soon noticed nothing was fresh and there was no odor of bear urine. Walking around a large boulder, his light picked up a reflection: Obsidian, that the Indians prized so much and then a sparkle of fool's gold. Fantasies flickered through his mind as he dreamed of finding that vein of gold two feet wide.

Suddenly he felt fresh air blowing on his face and he caught a whiff of pungent bear odor. He moved slowly and quietly further into the cave, swinging his light from side to side. Reacting to a sound, Kirk swung the light to the left just as the bear's gigantic paw came slamming down on his left shoulder. Kirk's rifle went off, hitting the bear in the right rear leg and spinning him away from Kirk.

Kirk, using his right leg as a brace and his good right arm, levered another shell in his rifle. The bear lunged at his attacker and his jaws closed around his left leg, breaking the bone. He picked Kirk up and shook him violently . Knowing this was his last chance, Kirk fired the rifle with the muzzle pressed against his enormous chest.

Kirk thought he had missed but slowly the bear began to slump as the damage of the hollow point bullet took its toll in its heart and lungs. Kirk hit the cave floor hard as the bear collapsed. It's jaw locked firmly on his left leg, Kirk passed out.

Later, when he awoke, he couldn't tell how long he'd been out. He could see a flicker from his flashlight off to his left. He tried to move his left arm and then his left leg but soon realized the bear still had him in his jaws. Pulling his large Bowie knife from his belt, he cut the bear's jaw muscles and pried open his mouth. Dragging himself free, he used a piece of rope as a tourniquet to stop the bleeding and then passed out again.

▲ ▲ ▲

"Marie, are you awake," asked the young doctor, as he gently shook her arm. Marie's eyes opened quickly. The question in her eyes said it all. The doctor smiled. "All your tests are negative. You're a healthy young woman and we'll have you out of here by the weekend."

▲ ▲ ▲

Coming to, Kirk knew he had to get to the mouth of the cave before his flashlight batteries ran out. He slowly opened his pack, retrieved a bottle of water, took six aspirin and ate a candy bar. Then he began to drag himself along the floor. Soon he could see light at the cave's entrance. As he got closer, he could hear the distant barking of dogs. If he could get a little closer, he could squeeze off three rounds from his .44 Magnum.

For two days five hunters and four dogs had been tracking the bear's blood trail. They had followed it up Hawley Creek Trail and across the mountain to Upside Down Trail and now the track was leading them up Baboon Mountain into the old caves and gold mine.

Kirk pulled out his gun, thinking I mustn't lose consciousness again, as he pulled the trigger.

The yellow grizzly had been ahead of the dogs for two days. They didn't really bother him, but he kept moving away from them as he headed for the caves where he grew up. The ripe smell of blood and humans hit his nose just as he entered the cave. The bullet from Kirk's .44 slammed into his chest, but he charged with lightening speed.

Kirk saw the bear's silhouette in the mouth of the cave and for a split second thought he was dreaming. But he instantly realized it was real as the large jaws closed on his thigh. He fired again as the huge bear picked him up and began slamming him against the wall. Kirk screamed and shot again. With that the bear let go of his leg and clamped down on his head. It cracked like a melon.

About that time, the dogs came to a screaming halt at the cave's entrance. They could hear the bear growling. Ben said, "I think I heard a scream and a shot."

"Get that lead dog on a leash, check your flashlights and rifles. Men, this is very dangerous. You don't have to go in. It's my job," Bill Grant said. His remarks were met with four big smiles. To a Montanan, this was fun.

They hadn't gone ten yards when their flashlights caught the gleam of the bear's eyes. It stopped feeding, looked up at the intruders with blood dripping from his muzzle.

"It's Kirk," Ben said, as his flashlight played over the checkered shirt.

"I'm authorizing a grizzly bear kill," Bill said, under his breath. All five safeties clicked as the 1,200 pound grizzly bear charged. Four shots went off in succession. The wounded bear slowed but didn't stop. The fifth shot broke his right hind leg, the sixth, his left. Breaking the bear down so he couldn't run, his charge still carried him within ten feet of the hunters.

After a few minutes, Bill stepped forward, touched the bear's muzzle and then his eye with his loaded, cocked rifle.

"He's dead."

Ben had gone ahead to check on Kirk, but he quickly realized it was way too late. There was blood on the floor, walls and ceiling of the cave, and only part of Kirk was there. As they were doing the messy job of putting what was left of Kirk into a body bag, Sam, the Deputy Sheriff said, "I hear from my friends in Depuyer that this guy was quite a wife beater. He won't be doing that again, that's for sure."

"Montana justice," Ben said.

EPILOGUE

The summer moved quickly into fall, and the ranch settled back into a normal routine. Wade hired a new cook who would stay on until the first of November. Marie spent a week in the hospital before moving into a girlfriend's apartment in Billings. After three weeks, she got a job as a cook in one of the local restaurants. Wade called several times, but someone was always around and Marie could never explain what happened. She tried to write him but just couldn't seem to get the words on paper.

After four phone calls Wade just gave up. He couldn't understand how Marie could have been so loving then and so distant now. Maybe he reminded her of her dead ex-husband. Or maybe she blamed him for his death. It must have been just a summer romance. Besides, he had to move on. He and Ben were closing the ranch next week and once the water and power were off, he would be leaving for a six week horse shoeing class in Dillon.

Cindy and Jake took the horses down to the winter pasture. They had talked as they rode the twenty-three miles down the road about getting jobs as wranglers together in Arizona. But as chance would have it, as soon as Cindy got to town the next day, she got a job taking care of Randy Thompson's horses for the winter. Jake took the job in Arizona. Anna gathered her

Forest Service husband up at the trail head and moved into their winter home in Bozeman with three of the ranch cats. Ben Johnson got a job in Oregon. Leigh and Pam went back to school looking forward to a new class of boys to train. They each promised Wade they would be back to work next summer.

The winter winds blew the dust off the road as the last vehicle started down the mountain and the snow began to fall lightly on the pasture. Deer and elk found shelter under the big Douglas firs. Spring was a long way off.

Months later, on one sunny April day, Marie left Billings thinking of the ranch. In a matter of hours, there she was all alone in the lodge looking out the picture windows remembering her summer. Her eyes swept the view and she was delighted to see the flowers starting to bloom and the green grass coming up beneath the snow. Taking a pencil and some paper from the kitchen, she wrote Wade a letter. In it she explained everything, her feelings, her heartache, her shame and most of all her love. She sealed the envelope and taped it to the refrigerator where it would wait for Wade. She walked through the door, thinking of the future and knowing she would be back.